DEADLY INHERITANCE

1927: Sarah Morton is looking forward to starting her new job as a tutor with a wealthy Yorkshire family, but she is taken aback when her young charge, Justin Howard, claims that someone wants him dead — and his great-grandfather seems to believe the same. Could greed be a motivating factor in the attempts to see off the young heir? And is Justin's handsome Uncle Adam really to be trusted?

PHYLLIS MALLETT

DEADLY INHERITANCE

Complete and Unabridged

LINFORD
Leicester

First published in Great Britain in 2004

First Linford Edition
published 2013

A catalogue record for this book is available
from the British Library.

ISBN 978–1–4448–1721–8

Published by
F. A. Thorpe (Publishing)
Anstey, Leicestershire

Set by Words & Graphics Ltd.
Anstey, Leicestershire
Printed and bound in Great Britain by
T. J. International Ltd., Padstow, Cornwall

This book is printed on acid-free paper

1

Sarah took a fresh grip on her case, which had seemed to become heavier with each passing moment, and strode on through the night with renewed resolution, her determination as firm as the moment she had set out from the railway station to walk the five miles to Shepton Manor.

It had been arranged by the agency that she would be met at the station by someone from the manor, but that hadn't happened, and her strong sense of independence had induced her to walk to her destination carrying the smaller of her two cases rather than cool her heels waiting for transport that might never arrive. But darkness had fallen within the hour and now rain was sluicing down; a few large drops at first which turned quickly to a heavy precipitation that soaked her as thoroughly as if she had fallen into a lake.

Her feet were squelching in her shoes, she was chilled and beginning to wish she had taken heed of her intuitive foreboding about going off into the wilds of Yorkshire to live among strangers.

Was this a sign of how her life was going to unfold now she had taken the big step of leaving London to make a fresh start in the Yorkshire Dales? She had cut herself off from the hurtful past, which included Colin, for he was history now, she reminded herself. He had been concerned only with the realities of life as it would affect him, whereas she had striven for the dream that evolved in her mind after her mother died.

The darkness was impenetrable. There were no lights anywhere to relieve the black void. A cold breeze was blowing into her face and the rain was now a pitiless downpour, drumming against the foliage of the trees lining the road and splashing up from the hard ground. It was the end of September, 1927, and autumn had come in with a vengeance.

At that moment a low growl sounded close by and she froze in shock as a heavy boot scraped on the ground almost at her side. Straining her eyes, she could see nothing more than a faint outline of a moving figure that loomed out of the darkness to confront her.

'Who's there?' she demanded shakily.

'Who are you?' a male voice countered instantly. 'What are you doing out here miles from anywhere?'

'Miles from anywhere?' she cried. 'But that cannot be. Surely I am close to Shepton Manor. At the railway station I was told it was about five miles to the manor, and I must have covered that distance by now. I seem to have been walking for hours.'

'The manor entrance is opposite. Do you have business there?'

Surprise edged the anonymous voice. 'I do.' Sarah's relief was boundless.

She was not lost after all. 'I have been engaged as a tutor by Mister Howard Kane for his great grandson. It was arranged that I would be met at the station but that didn't happen, so I've walked, and it's a good thing I decided to because I haven't been passed by any kind of transport since I set out. They must have forgotten this is the day of my arrival.'

The man uttered a short laugh.

'Really. I wasn't told about you, and that's probably why you weren't met. I'm the one who does everything around here, for if I don't then nothing would get done. But I've been kept in the dark about you. It is scandalous that you were not met, and it's a good thing I chanced along at this moment or you might have walked all the way to Shepton. What's your name?'

'Sarah Morton. Whom am I addressing?'

'Adam Kane.' He chuckled somewhat harshly, and a strong hand came out of the darkness and relieved Sarah of the burdensome case. 'This way. You must be very tired, and this case is exceptionally heavy. Did you pack the kitchen sink by mistake?'

Sarah laughed, unsure of herself because the anonymous voice had not the slightest hint of friendliness in it.

She blinked as a yellow beam of light suddenly illuminated the ground in front of them, and she saw Adam Kane's velveteen-covered legs and the head of a large sheepdog that was by his side. He had opened a covered lantern he was carrying, and she was relieved to be able to see at last. The dancing rays of the lantern bobbed and swayed through the shadows as they left the road and passed between black iron gates set between two massive brick pillars.

'So you've been engaged as a tutor for my nephew, Justin, eh? Well, I wish you luck, for I suspect you will need it. You'll have your work cut out, I fear. Justin is eleven years old. He's been a big problem since his father — my brother, Gilbert — died four years ago. And his mother died two years ago. Since then Justin has been well nigh unmanageable.

'He's had three tutors since my grandfather decided on that method of education, and one of them was a man who suddenly decided that he couldn't cope and left overnight, so I don't hold much hope of a female handling the job. Justin has been running wild. I've been pushing for him to be sent to a boarding school, but no headmaster is prepared to tolerate his behaviour.'

Sarah listened with growing consternation, for this situation had not been explained to her when she was offered the position at the manor. She realised now that she should have insisted on visiting Shepton Manor before deciding to accept the position, but it was too late for second thoughts. She was committed, and would have to make the best of the situation.

They emerged from under the trees and Adam lifted his lantern high to cast uncertain light through the shadows.

'I doubt you can see anything,' he remarked, 'but this is Shepton Manor, home of the Kane family for more than three centuries. I run the estate — I was out watching for poachers. They're a big problem at this time.'

They were ascending a flight of stone steps to a terrace as he spoke, and he reached out and pulled a metal handle beside the heavy oak door forming the entrance to the manor. A bell tolled sonorously, and moments later the door was unbarred and opened, and they were bathed in a shaft of yellow light that issued through the doorway.

Sarah's gaze went immediately to her companion and she saw a very tall man, broad-shouldered and powerfully built. His face was shadowed by the brim of his hat, but she noted that he was exceedingly handsome, his features ruggedly well formed. He would be in his late twenties, she judged.

'Wenn, this is Miss Morton, the new tutor, who is expected by some, I believe.' Adam Kane glanced at her, his face expressionless. 'See to her immediately. She has walked here from the railway station.'

'Miss Morton?' The man shook his head. Dressed as a butler, he was short and heavily built, his voice rasping. 'I didn't know she was due to arrive today. At least, I wasn't told.'

'I know nothing of her either, but here she is, so get her inside and settle her for the night. Matilda must have known something of Grandfather's plans. I shall want an account of who failed to pass on to me the information of her arrival, and there will be trouble over it, I assure you.'

'If Matilda knows anything then she didn't see fit to take me into her confidence, Mister Adam.' Wenn took Sarah's case from Adam's hand before stepping aside to admit her.

Sarah turned to thank Adam for his help but he was already moving away across the terrace, and she compressed her lips and stepped across the threshold into a large hall that had a floor of black and white marble tiles. The dim light from several wall sconces threw dense shadows into the corners and high ceiling, but she could see a number of doors set in dark oak-panelled walls that were lined with many portraits, all the faces of which stared impassively at her from the past.

'I'm Wenn, the butler, miss.' There was a conciliatory tone in the harsh voice, and Sarah was subjected to a close scrutiny that missed nothing of her tall, slim figure, soft features and alert blue eyes. 'My wife is housekeeper here. I'm sorry you've had such an ordeal, and I cannot understand why we were not informed that you would be arriving today. I shall take up the matter with Mister Howard, the master, but first I'll show you to the room that has been used for Master Justin's tutors in the past and you can change out of your wet clothes.

'I expect the master will want to see you as soon as I've reported your arrival. Please hold yourself ready to meet him. I was of the opinion, when I heard that you had been engaged, sight unseen, that it would have been to the mutual advantage of you and the Kane family if you were taken on a month's trial. That would have been the sensible thing to do, but I am afraid that sensibility is a rare commodity in this house.'

'I'm sure I shall manage to carry out my duties to the satisfaction of all concerned,' Sarah replied.

She glanced down at herself. Water was dripping upon the tiles from her coat. She felt exhausted, bedraggled, but was beyond caring what she looked like, and followed the butler as he walked to the staircase and ascended. A tall figure emerged from the shadows at the rear of the hall and relieved Wenn of the suitcase, then followed them silently up the imposing staircase.

'Try not to stand on polished floors anywhere in the house,' Wenn advised, 'or you'll make a mortal enemy of

Matilda. She carries her sense of house pride to an extreme. One would think she owned the manor, the way she runs it. But that comes from having been too long in the position and making herself indispensable.'

They reached the top of the stairs and walked along a wide, richly-carpeted corridor that was dimly illuminated by candles in wall sconces. A number of doors opened off on either side, Sarah noted, and they continued through an archway, after which the corridor narrowed and there was no carpet on the polished floorboards.

Wenn paused at the first door on the left and thrust it open to reveal a large room that was austerely finished with plain, whitewood furniture. A tall window, heavily curtained, covered most of the opposite wall, and Sarah experienced a shiver of relief when she saw a log fire burning merrily in the large grate, for it brought home to her the degree of discomfort she was feeling. A lamp on a table filled the room with dim light.

'Thank you, Frank,' Wenn took the suitcase from the silent footman, who withdrew immediately. The butler motioned for her to enter the room. 'Someone must have been expecting you or the fire wouldn't have been lit,' he observed. 'I expect this will be your room while you are here. The door on the left leads into Master Justin's room, and you would do well to keep it locked at all times — he's such a terror. Also, it would be a good thing to get into the habit of locking the door of this room whenever you leave it.'

Wenn turned to depart, his fleshy face set in a mask of indifference, his dark eyes glinting in the lamplight. He paused in the doorway and nodded slowly.

'I wish you well but I don't hold any great hopes for your success. Master Justin needs a strong man to handle him. He has to be disciplined, and I doubt you will have the authority to deal with him in the necessary manner. I shall send Janet, the maid, up for you in thirty minutes. You will need to see the master as soon as possible. I have been briefed on what your duties here will be, and the matter of your standing with the family. You are to be treated not as a servant but as a member of the family.'

Sarah sighed heavily when the door finally closed behind Wenn, and shook her head as she relaxed and looked around.

Crossing to the door that connected with Justin's room, she reached out a tentative hand to open it but changed her mind and instead pressed her ear against the panel. Hearing nothing, she shook her head as she considered the butler's opinion of her job. He had sounded like the knell of doom, and she had become concerned about what might lie ahead.

She opened a door in the right-hand wall and discovered the bathroom. Her nerves were over-stretched by tension, and as she walked into the bathroom a large black cat sprang at her like a vicious streak, miaowing furiously.

Sarah uttered a scream of shock and flung herself aside in a reflex action, not realising that the animal was a cat until it had passed her. It disappeared under her bed, and Sarah sagged in the doorway of the bathroom as she fought to recover her nerve, her heart pounding erratically.

At that moment the door to Justin's room was jerked open and a small, slight figure appeared in the doorway. Dark eyes gazed intently at Sarah as she recorded the physical appearance of Justin Kane. He was small for his age, with a shock of unruly black hair and intense brown eyes. Defiance was etched in his expression and a smirk was stamped upon his lips. His left arm was in a sling, the hand heavily bandaged.

'So you're the new tutor.' He spoke dispassionately, and waved the hand in the sling. 'I wouldn't bother to unpack your case, if I were you. I don't think you will be staying long. Have you seen my cat, by the way? She seems to prefer this room to mine. I'm forever having to fetch her out.'

'There was a cat imprisoned in my bathroom.' Sarah made an effort to appear unconcerned. 'A very extraordinary cat, if it is able to open and close doors. But apparently it didn't like the experience of being locked in. It's now hiding under the bed. You're Justin Kane, I assume.'

He did not reply, and she watched him get down to look under the bed. He flattened himself on the carpet and reached for the animal crouching there, which hissed ferociously as he drew it out by the scruff of its neck.

'You're very naughty, Arabella,' he scolded, a faint smile touching his lips. 'You're almost as bad as me.' He looked at Sarah from under indrawn brows, his dark eyes filled with calculation. 'I was told about you, Sarah Morton, and it's a pity you've had your journey from

London for nothing because you won't be able to teach me anything.' His smile was filled with defiance.

'Why not?' Sarah responded. 'You look intelligent enough to be able to learn if you applied yourself to the task. What have you done to your arm?'

'Someone tried to kill me last week.'

Justin turned and walked to the door of his room, and Sarah ran after him, stepping into the doorway as he turned to close the door.

'What did you say?' She was horrified by his words. 'Someone tried to kill you?'

'And not for the first time,' he added.

'Are you serious?'

'I don't expect you to believe me any more than anyone else in the house does. They all say it's another of my fairy tales.'

'What happened? Tell me about it.' Sarah was shocked by his matter-of-fact tone, but assumed that he was not telling the truth.

'There's nothing to tell.' He shrugged

his slim shoulders. 'I was playing at the back of the house and an ornamental urn weighing about a hundredweight fell off the parapet of the roof. It brushed my arm so I'm lucky to be alive. But I saw someone up on the roof, although I couldn't recognise the figure. All I saw was a black outline that moved. The sun was directly behind the figure, and dazzled me when I looked up.'

Sarah studied his face while her mind grappled with the shock of his utterance. Was he telling the truth or could this be a part of some juvenile plan to get rid of her?

'We'll talk tomorrow,' she decided. 'I have to see your great-grandfather shortly, and I need to change my clothes.'

Justin regarded her with lack-lustre eyes, his face expressionless. The cat, held tightly under his uninjured arm, was also gazing at her, a savage light in its strikingly green eyes, and their general attitude seemed to set the tone of the welcome that Sarah was receiving. She closed the door, and a cold shudder passed through her as she turned the key in the lock, for it was possible that Justin had been telling the truth about his injury.

What had she let herself in for? Her first impressions were uncertain, and when there was a knock at the door of the room she steeled herself for what might prove to be an ordeal — her meeting with the Kane family.

2

A tall girl dressed in the dark uniform of a maid was standing in the corridor when Sarah opened the door of her room. Heavy of build, with a big, fleshy face and piercing brown eyes, she had the ruddy cheeks of a country girl and smiled pleasantly as she bobbed quickly in a parody of a curtsey.

'Good evening, miss. I'm Janet. If you're ready now, I'll take you down to Mister Howard's study.'

'Thank you, Janet. I'm Sarah Morton.'

Sarah paused as she recalled the butler's advice about locking her door, but decided against it and followed the maid along the corridor.

'You're very pretty for a tutor,' Janet observed, 'and young. The tutors who were here before were frumpish, except the man.' She laughed. 'I wish I had fair hair like yours. I'm twenty-four, and

19

you can't be much older. Frank Turner told me you had to walk from the station. Didn't they know you were arriving today, miss?'

'I was under the impression they did.' Sarah was warmed slightly by the maid's girlish chatter. Here was someone who seemed normal and friendly. 'Who is Frank Turner?'

'He's the footman. He carried your case up to your room. Be careful of Frank. He thinks he's a lady-killer, but he's obnoxious — always trying to attract the tutors we've had for young Justin. Mrs Wenn will be to blame for your not being met at the station. She's the go-between for us and the family. All their orders come through her. She rules the staff with a rod of iron. Have you had much experience teaching children?'

'Yes, indeed.'

'Well, I hope you get on well with Master Justin. He's a terror all right. But that's only to be expected, the things that have happened in his young life. I do feel sorry for him even though he plagues the life out of me. I think he's a very lonely child, and no-one has cared for him since his mother died.'

They reached the staircase, and Sarah saw a tall, middle-aged woman, dressed in a severe black dress, standing at the foot of the stairs and looking upward, regarding her with glinting brown eyes set in an angular face that was grimly expressioned.

Iron-grey hair was drawn back into a bun. A large bunch of keys was dangling from a black belt girding the small waist.

'Janet,' she called imperiously, 'I hope you're not gossiping. It wouldn't do to give Miss Morton a wrong impression about the manor.'

'No, Mrs Wenn. I was merely explaining the lay-out of the house.'

Sarah compressed her lips. So this was the butler's wife. She could feel the housekeeper's piercing gaze upon her as she descended the stairs, and suffered a close inspection until they were face to face.

'I'm Matilda Wenn, the housekeeper, and you'll be Sarah Morton.' There was no warmth in the tone. 'Welcome to Shepton Manor. I hope your stay here will be fruitful.'

'Thank you. I'm sure it will. Have you heard that I had to walk from the station?' There was a challenge in Sarah's tone. 'I was under the impression that I would be met.'

'I'm very sorry about that. I was not informed that you would be arriving today. I don't know what went wrong, but I shall find out, you may be sure. Now, I'll show you to Mister Howard's study. He's waiting to meet you. Later, I'll take you to meet Justin himself. This way, if you please.' She paused and turned her attention to Janet, who was standing submissively on the bottom stair. 'Have you nothing to do?' she demanded sharply.

Janet departed quickly and Sarah followed the upright figure of the housekeeper along a corridor to the right. Mrs Wenn did not speak again and Sarah was not inclined to break the intimidating silence.

The housekeeper paused at a door on the left and knocked, then opened the door and ushered Sarah into the room.

'Miss Sarah Morton, Mr Howard,' she announced, and turned to depart immediately, her dark eyes glinting, the hint of an ironic smile showing on her thin, uncompromising lips. She closed the door, leaving Sarah alone on the threshold of a book-lined room facing a very old man who was seated in an armchair to one side of a blazing log fire burning in the grate.

'Come forward, Miss Morton, that I may see you clearly. My sight is not what it used to be.'

Howard Kane paused and subjected Sarah to a close scrutiny as she crossed the room.

Sarah's first impression was of extreme age. His face was a mass of small wrinkles and sagging flesh dominated by a high-bridged nose. Above the nose the eyes were dark and inscrutable, and beneath it his mouth was down-curved, looking like that of a dead cod on a fishmonger's slab.

'Forgive me if I appear to have forgotten my manners,' he apologised. 'I have arthritis, among other things, and my joints don't behave very well at times. But, at the age of eighty-three, I cannot complain, although I constantly yearn for the return of my youth. The onset of yet another autumn is punishing me, but what cannot be cured must be endured. I'm so very glad you have arrived, and I sincerely hope that you will have a steadying effect on Justin.'

'I shall do my very best to help him.' Sarah was studying Howard Kane's appearance. He did not look to be a well man, was frail, and his hands shook at times, although he made great efforts to control them.

'My great grandson has become an intolerable burden,' he said wearily, motioning Sarah to a seat opposite and pausing until she had sat down. 'I'm at my wits' end, not knowing what to do for the best. Justin has had a number of tutors, none of whom has been satisfactory, and I've come to the conclusion that the key to handling him is old-fashioned caring. In fact, I would like you to try that course when setting out your plan for his education.

'I was impressed by your qualifications, and your references are impeccable. But, for the time being, I would prefer you to treat Justin as a companion rather than a pupil. I'm convinced that's why your predecessors failed. They tried the customary practice of disciplined education, with my approval, I might add.

'However you can lead a horse to water but you cannot make it drink. So at the outset, would you rely on my assessment of Justin's problem and handle him the way I suggest? Forget about lessons and try to bring him out of the attitude he's adopted. If you can improve his behaviour and break down the hurdle he seems to have erected in his mind then he might become amenable to education.'

'Certainly,' Sarah agreed instantly. 'It would be difficult, If not impossible, to teach an intractable pupil, so I'm inclined to believe that Justin's confidence has first to be won. If you'll give me some details of his background it will enable me to make an assessment and set out a curriculum. I would, of course, confer with you at each stage, and I should think that together we can bring Justin back to normal childhood.'

'If only it could be that easy.' Howard Kane shook his head. 'And I must apologise for not giving my household more information about your coming. All they knew was that a new tutor had been engaged but not when you would take up your duties. That is the reason why you were not met at the station. I fear I tried to be too clever. I wanted to get the reactions of my family to your unannounced arrival and, by forgetting to have you met, I turned the whole situation against myself. Now they suspect me of manipulating everyone for some nefarious reason.'

'I am afraid I don't understand.' Sarah was still keenly aware of the long walk she had been compelled to make.

'When you have met the members of my family you might begin to realise something of the problems I face.' His eyes bored into Sarah as if intending to strip away flesh itself as he endeavoured to assess her character while approving her air of professionalism. 'I want you to regard yourself as a member of my family while you are here, and, above all, maintain a close watch over Justin as far as you can.'

'I have already met your grandson. He introduced himself when I entered my room.' Sarah smiled at the memory.

'Really? What kind of a reception did he arrange for you?' Howard's face suddenly registered alarm. 'I hope it was nothing serious — like a grass snake in your bed! That's what Richard Compton, the tutor before last, alleged when he first arrived. And all the other tutors complained repeatedly of Justin's bad behaviour.'

'It wasn't that serious.' Sarah smiled. 'A boyish prank. Perhaps Justin is relenting already. He has an injured arm, I noticed. Was he involved in an accident?'

'He was, and a very serious one. A decorative urn, one of many adorning the parapet of the roof, toppled to the ground, almost hitting Justin. It was a miracle he was not killed. I've had the whole building checked, just in case. But the manor is in a good state of repair. The builder reported that the urn which had fallen was the only one in a weakened condition, but I ordered them all to be removed. One cannot be too careful.

'I am wondering how well you have been briefed by your agency, although I did not tell them about the situation which I suspect exists here. I merely stressed the qualities I expected in the person they planned to send, and they suggested you immediately. I hope you will be able to handle any situation that is likely to crop up in our work with Justin, however grave it may prove to be. But it may be asking too much of a woman.'

'You had better explain,' Sarah suggested. 'Take me fully into your confidence and I should be able to deal with any problems that arise.'

'Of course. Justin is the only son of my eldest grandson, William, who died in Africa four years ago, and Justin's mother died two years later, of a broken heart, I suspect. I have two other grandsons and a married grand-daughter living in the household.

'Adam is older than Owen by two years, and Elizabeth, four years older than Adam, has her husband, Francis Fernley, living here with her. Fernley is an artist — at least he makes a living from what he paints.

'I would prefer you to get to know my family in the normal way and form your own opinion of their merits and attitudes. I ought not burden you with too much at this time. But we must get together regularly to discuss whatever you discover in the course of your duties. Always remember not to accept anything at face value. And please bear in mind that my door is open to you at any time of the day or night.'

'I'm getting the impression that you would have me spy on your family.'

Sarah looked into dark eyes that seemed to be bore right through her.

'That is putting it a little too strongly.' He sighed and shook his head. 'I expect you to do whatever lies in your power to safeguard Justin's safety. He seems to be in peril, the details of which are not plain to me at the moment. A number of incidents involving him have occurred which cannot all be pure misadventure.'

Sarah nodded, not knowing what to think. His words filled her with a cold fear as she considered the implications, and she wondered what on earth she had walked into.

'Why would someone want to harm Justin?' she asked.

Howard Kane sighed and shook his head.

'One word would sum it up — greed. Legally, Justin, being the only son of an eldest son of an eldest son, will inherit Shepton Manor when I pass on, and I fear that someone in the family is planning to change the normal course of inheritance. That is mainly my reason for hiring you. I cannot get Justin into a boarding school while his behaviour is so unsociable, and I should be afraid to let him go if it were otherwise. I need to expose whoever is imperilling his life.

'It is a tremendous task for you to undertake, and I am sorry for its necessity. Please do tell me if you feel unable to cope with the responsibility, and I will see that you leave tomorrow, suitably recompensed for your trouble.'

'I'll stay.'

Sarah spoke without hesitation, for an image of Justin Kane's face lay in the centre of a dark cloud of foreboding which had formed in her mind.

'Very good.' He smiled. 'I'm relieved by your decision. Now what else can I say that will aid you? Owen is delicate physically, and susceptible to every malady that cares to visit him. He took over the day-to-day running of the estate when Justin's father died because I had become too infirm, but resigned in favour of Adam, who went to sea as soon as he was old enough to travel and was compelled to return home and assume responsibility, although he was never cut out to be a farmer.

'My granddaughter, Elizabeth, lives here ostensibly to care for Justin, but she has never showed the slightest interest in him. She was living in Cornwall with her husband until Justin's mother died, when she decided to return here and care for the boy. But I detect no feelings in her for him. And Justin must be aware of her attitude because he reacts quite strongly against her. There's never been any love lost between them.

'Now, I have taken up too much of your time. I'm sure you have much to do to settle in. I've instructed Janet to take care of you, and don't hesitate to acquaint her with your needs. You will answer to no-one in the household but me. Dinner is at eight o'clock, so return here at a few minutes to the hour and I'll escort you into the dining-room and introduce you to my family.'

'Thank you.' Sarah arose and departed to return to her room, her mind seething with what she had learned. She had been looking forward to a normal teaching position, but this promised to be anything but straight-forward, and could she handle such a situation?

Opening the door to her room, she paused in consternation, for her clothes had been removed from her case and strewn around haphazardly, crumpled and thrown down as if by a malicious, childish hand, and she recalled Wenn's advice about locking the door whenever she left the room.

She looked towards the connecting door that gave access to Justin's room and noticed that it was ajar. A frown came to her face as she crossed to it and pushed it wide. But Justin was absent, and she looked around uncertainly. As far as she knew, his movements were under no restraint, but in view of Howard Kane's suspicions, she felt that she should be aware of Justin's whereabouts at all times.

Returning to her room, she attended to the task of hanging her clothes in the wardrobe, but there was an uneasiness in her mind when she checked Justin's room at five minutes to eight and found no sign of the boy.

She hurried down to Howard Kane's study to report, and relief filled her when she entered and saw Justin there with his great-grandfather. The boy regarded her impassively, his eyes filled with unfriendliness.

'Punctual to the minute,' Howard Kane approved, arising with difficulty from his seat. 'Justin, walk ahead and open the doors for us, there's a good boy. Justin and I have been chatting, Sarah, and I've elicited a promise from him to be on his best behaviour. I've told him there will be no dreary lessons until you've settled in, and he is to regard the next week as something of a holiday. We must start as we mean to go on, and Justin has been made aware that any reproduction of his former bad behaviour will be severely dealt with.'

'I'm sure we can look forward to a pleasant future,' Sarah responded, adjusting her stride to Howard's infirm walk.

Justin walked ahead of them, his shoulders stiff, and he did not look around until they reached the hall, when he glanced at them briefly as he paused at a door, remaining motionless until they reached him. Then he flung open the door so violently it crashed against the wall and rebounded, to be stopped by his well-placed foot.

Howard remonstrated, but Sarah was gazing into the dining-room at the three men and a woman already seated at the long table and gazing expectantly towards the door. They had been talking animatedly until Justin thrust open the door — Sarah had picked up the hum of their voices. Now they were poised for their first glimpse of her, and Sarah was aware of tension seeping into her chest as she accompanied Howard Kane into the long room, wondering exactly what she had let herself in for.

'This is Miss Sarah Morton,' Howard announced, and proceeded to introduce Sarah to the members of his family. 'My granddaughter, Elizabeth, and her husband, Francis Fernley.'

'How do you do, Mrs Fernley?'

'Please call me Elizabeth. No need to stand on ceremony here. If you've come to live as one of the family then formality would be most tiresome. I shall call you Sarah. This is Francis, my husband. I don't envy you the task you have taken on, Sarah. That boy is a fiend in human guise.'

She glared at Justin with dislike in her brown eyes.

'Justin, close the door now and come to your place,' Howard said firmly. 'Sarah, that's Adam down at the far end of the table. Owen is nearer the fire.'

Both men had risen to their feet at Sarah's entrance and were gazing at her. There was a faint expression on Adam's handsome face that Sarah took to be boredom, and his lips were pinched as he nodded. He was tall, dark-haired, cheeks clean-shaven, his brown eyes filled with a glint that made her wonder at the slant of his thoughts.

'How do you do, Miss Morton?' Adam acknowledged. 'I trust you have recovered from your hike.'

'Yes, thank you,' she responded.

He smiled faintly and sat down. Sarah turned her attention to Owen, who was regarding her steadily. Two years younger than Adam, he seemed much less robust, but appeared to be the friendliest as he acknowledged her with a nod and a smile before sitting down, his keen gaze flickering over her, noting her plain, dark dress and the single strand of pearls around her neck.

'Ah, the mysterious young lady who descended upon us unannounced.'

Sarah looked quickly at the speaker. Francis Fernley had not risen at her entrance. He was a handsome man, probably in his middle thirties, and exuded an aura of remoteness as he leaned back in his chair and studied her through half-closed eyelids.

'You will have a very interesting time here,' he observed.

'Come and sit beside me.'

Howard Kane took Sarah's arm and led her to the table, gripping her wrist firmly as if trying to implant confidence in her mind.

Sarah smiled, endeavouring to exhibit an appearance of calm indifference to the tension that seemed to envelop the room, but felt strangely uneasy about this strange household she had joined.

3

Sarah took advantage of the pause afforded by being seated at the table to look around the impressive dining-room. A massive crystal chandelier was suspended from a beautifully-scrolled ceiling and, facing her, a long glass cabinet contained silver and crystal objects which were alive with imprisoned light that changed colour at the slightest movement of her head.

She glanced over her shoulder at an enormous sideboard, upon which Frank Turner, the footman, under the silent supervision of Wenn, was in the act of placing steaming dishes containing the first course of the meal.

Keenly aware of being the cynosure of all eyes, and although Elizabeth kept the conversation moving, Sarah found it difficult to maintain her end of it because she could sense undercurrents of emotions and attitudes that kept surfacing around the table.

Elizabeth also attacked Howard, but in a disarming way, smiling as she questioned his intentions and reasons for engaging yet another tutor, but picking at him intently, like a dog attacking a bone.

'I cannot understand why you kept Sarah's arrival secret, Grandfather,' she chided, a barb concealed in her well-modulated voice. 'And then you forgot to have her met at the station. And, Sarah, why did you not get the stationmaster to telephone the manor and report your arrival? I feel that you displayed bad judgement, and if you make a habit of that failing you can be sure Justin will take advantage of it.'

Sarah recognised the rebuke delivered by the soft voice but steeled herself against replying. Howard, however, spoke quite sharply in an attempt to shield her from further attack, but only succeeded in turning the conversation from idle chatter into something much more serious.

'I don't have to account to you, Elizabeth, or anyone, for my reasons and decisions,' he said tartly. 'For a long time now I've had a suspicion that none of you is really interested in family affairs. Owen is filled with his own misery. Adam is not at all happy pursuing the responsibilities of his employment — he would rather do anything but run the estate. And you, Elizabeth, could have remained in Cornwall for all the assistance you afford me. I am alone in my predicament — caring for Justin — and the Lord knows how I shall proceed if Sarah falls in the task I have set her.'

'You're being unduly harsh, Grandfather,' Adam observed. 'I, for one, have done all I can to help, and I've made no complaint about having to run the estate when you could so easily employ a manager more suited to the responsibilities of day-to-day administration.'

'And you will persist in blaming me

for my ill health,' Owen said more sharply, his dark eyes glinting. 'Perhaps you would like me to go out and labour in the fields like a farm hand to prove my loyalty.'

'I came back from Cornwall quite willingly, Grandfather.' Elizabeth's voice brooked no opposition and silenced her brothers. 'I mean to do my bit for the family, and Francis has made a big personal sacrifice by coming with me. But Justin is an ungrateful wretch who has us all in the throes of worry and despair while he thinks up even more ways to make us suffer.'

Sarah glanced at Justin, who was sitting on the other side of Howard, and was struck by the fact that he showed no interest or emotion in the conversation flowing around him. When dinner was served he fell to eating as if he were sitting alone, his eyes on his plate, every facet of expression indicating that he had closed his mind to what was going on around him.

By now Owen, seeming to eat very

little, directed questions at her in a steady stream, all of which required an answer, and she found herself revealing details of her past life under his determined interrogation while the others listened intently to her replies.

'Have you ever lived in the country before, Sarah?' he demanded.

'Never, and I'm really looking forward to the experience,' she replied.

'But won't you miss the bright lights and the company? One has to experience the remoteness here to fully appreciate how awful it is. There is just nothing to do, and boredom is a real problem.'

'I have always been too busy to be able to spend much time on leisure pursuits so I certainly won't miss them.' Sarah kept her tone even.

The questions continued until Howard interrupted.

'I think that is enough for now, Owen,' he said sharply. 'Sarah will be thinking that she has made a mistake in coming here. I suggest you all adopt my approach and wait to see how she handles the situation.'

He glanced at the silent Justin, then reached out and ruffled the boy's hair.

'You're going to be on your best behaviour, aren't you?'

'I don't need a tutor,' Justin replied. 'No-one can teach me anything.'

He scowled at Sarah and resumed his mask of impassivity.

A lull ensued, and the silence seemed even worse than the questioning. Sarah realised that she was unusually tense, and made an effort to relax, hoping that this ordeal of barely-concealed disapproval by the family would not be repeated at future mealtimes.

But she was aware that Francis Fernley, who took no part in the general conversation, was regarding her with sympathy in his expression and, whenever their glances chanced to meet, his impassive features relaxed slightly to reveal a cautious smile. But Elizabeth maintained a barely concealed edge of unfriendliness, and although Adam showed hardly any emotion at all she sensed that he was not enamoured by her presence.

As the meal ended, Howard pushed back his chair and arose unsteadily.

'I'm sure you will excuse me,' he said firmly. 'I am feeling rather tired. The meal has been something of an ordeal, and in future you would do well to better conceal your feelings.

'Sarah, I shall want to talk to you in my study first thing in the morning. Say, eight-thirty. Justin, escort me to my room and then return here for Sarah. I charge you with attending to your new tutor and administering to her needs, however small.' He paused and regarded the boy with an intent gaze, forcing Justin to look up at him. 'Do you understand?' he demanded.

'Yes, Grandfather,' Justin answered, and his gaze slid to Sarah, his dark eyes carrying a warning that all would not be well between them.

The tension around the table seemed to diminish when Howard had departed.

Owen poured wine into his glass and sighed deeply as he leaned back in his chair and made an effort to relax.

'That was an ordeal I shouldn't want to repeat,' Adam observed. He smiled at Sarah. 'But Grandfather is always on the offensive when we have a new tutor for Justin. I do hope the atmosphere didn't deter you, Sarah. If you can work a miracle with Justin then all will be well. And you can count on each of us to help all we can, so don't hesitate to call if the need for aid should arise.

'It seems to me that Grandfather has painted a dark picture for you, but I'm sure it won't be as bad as he insists. We're all greatly concerned about Justin, but we have experienced his attitudes for a long time, and we're of the opinion that he is incorrigible and you will soon go the way of your predecessors.'

'You make Justin sound like an ogre,' Sarah observed. 'But I do not attach much importance to what has gone before. I shall do my best, and feel certain that Justin will react favourably.'

'I admire your courage.' Adam smiled faintly. 'But I fear your hopes will be dashed the moment you attempt to discipline Justin. I shall be interested in your progress, and please consider me an ally if you should need help.' He stood up suddenly. 'I must go now. I still have some work to do before I can call it a day.'

'You make too much of the job,' Owen observed coldly. 'You're always complaining about how much you have to do. Personally, I never found that much to do when I ran the estate.'

'That's why the place slipped into trouble,' Adam retorted. 'Your lack of attention to detail enabled endless problems to arise.'

Adam departed, and Sarah welcomed the easing of tension. She sighed with relief when Elizabeth arose from the table and strode from the room, but the woman paused in the doorway and turned to address her husband, who was filling his glass and looked to be preparing to spend time drinking with Owen.

'Don't drink too much, Francis,' she warned. 'We have a busy day tomorrow and need to be up before daylight. Good-night, Sarah, and good luck. I think you'll need it.'

'Good-night,' Sarah responded. She pushed back her chair but did not rise, and looked around the long room.

'Do you wish to return to your room?' Justin asked solemnly.

'Not yet, unless it is time for you to go to bed,' she replied. 'Perhaps you would care to conduct me on a tour of the manor.'

Sarah arose and walked to the door without comment, and Justin went ahead of her, opening the door and standing aside for her to exit. He slammed the door resoundingly after following her into the corridor. She made no comment, and followed him as he crossed the hall and opened the nearest door.

'The library,' he announced. 'This is

where I take my lessons, when I have them.'

Sarah glanced at him, expecting to see a smile on his face, but no emotion showed, and his eyes were cold, containing a remoteness that boded ill for the future.

An air of peace filled Sarah as she looked around. Feeling at home immediately, she smiled and turned to Justin, who had closed the door and was standing with his back to it, his gaze directed at a spot on the green carpet just in front of his feet. He did not meet her gaze although she paused to give him an opportunity to speak.

'This is a beautiful room,' she observed. 'We shall be very happy working in here. Tell me, what are your favourite subjects?'

'I don't have any.' He walked to the fireplace and stood with his back to the burning coals, regarding Sarah impassively, and she wondered at the way his life must have progressed to this present attitude. Both his parents were dead, and she assumed the double tragedy was having a great influence upon him.

But there had to be a key to his behaviour, she was aware, and fished for a lever to get at it. If she could unravel that secret she could draw him out and bring him back to normal.

The silence lengthened as Sarah walked to the nearest cabinet and examined the titles of the books.

'Do you read much?' she enquired, not looking at Justin.

He did not reply and she continued to ignore his presence while she wondered how best to approach him. The silence became overpowering. Sarah turned to take a firmer line with him, and gaped in astonishment when she saw that he was no longer in the room.

'Justin,' she called urgently, looking around wildly, certain that he could not have reached the door without alerting her. 'Where are you?'

She walked the length of the room,

looking to see if he had secreted himself behind the drawn curtains or hidden behind the desk, and her perplexity grew when she found no sign of him.

Sarah left the library and crossed to the dining-room. Owen was still seated at the table, and he smiled when she entered.

'What have you done with Justin?' he demanded, reaching out to refill his glass. 'Have you drowned him already?'

'We were in the library and he seems to have vanished into thin air,' Sarah said. 'I suspect he made use of a secret exit, or something.'

Owen pushed himself to his feet, chuckling softly.

'I shall have to take you on a tour of the house and point out all the places where Justin can take his leave of you secretly. If you're aware of his tricks it will at least give you a chance of beating him at his own game.'

He led the way back into the library, and Sarah halted in midstride because Justin was standing before the fire. He regarded them impassively, although his eyes were filled with glistening emotion.

'Grandfather has warned you against playing tricks, Justin,' Owen said. 'Why do you persist in treating your tutors as enemies when they have come here only to help you?'

'I don't like strangers in the house,' Justin observed. 'I think a tutor should come in the morning and leave when lessons are over.'

'You're an absolute horror!' Owen walked to the right of the fireplace, pressed a projection in the exotically-patterned woodwork, and a section of bookcase swung inwards to reveal a cavity beyond. 'Come and look,' he invited Sarah, and she crossed to his side. 'It's a priest-hole,' he explained, and she looked into a small cell-like room that was completely bare. 'There are a number of these around the house, and Justin has made it his business to locate them.'

Owen operated the catch several times, and showed Sarah exactly where to press to operate it. She looked towards the fireplace, and was in time to see Justin departing from the room. He closed the door with a customary slam.

'He's starting as he means to go on,' Owen observed. 'Life will be filled with traumas and tensions from now on. I can promise that you will know no peace until you've had your fill and decide to leave.'

Sarah opened her mouth to reply but was interrupted by the sound of a high-pitched scream which was followed immediately by a horrifying crash that echoed through the house.

4

Sarah reached the foot of the staircase behind Owen and paused when she saw Janet, the maid, lying crumpled on the bottom stair. Beside the apparently unconscious girl was a suit of armour that had been standing on a plinth on the landing above. Owen bent over Janet as Wenn appeared from the servants' quarters. The butler came to Sarah's side, his fleshy face filled with enquiry, his brown eyes narrowed to take in the scene.

'I heard a scream,' Wenn observed. 'What happened?'

Sarah shook her head.

'We don't know, but it looks as if that suit of armour fell off its plinth as Janet descended the stairs.'

'Fell?' Wenn shook his head. 'Impossible! A grown man couldn't move that armour.'

Owen was chafing Janet's wrists and

his ministrations began to have an effect because the girl stirred and lifted her head. She gazed up at Owen, her eyes blank, and then her memory returned and she clutched at Owen's hands.

'Oh, Mister Owen,' she gasped. 'I was coming downstairs when I heard a noise from behind. I looked back to see that suit of armour toppling off its plinth. It came crashing down the stairs. I was able to get out of its way, but lost my balance and fell.'

'It's all right, Janet,' Owen spoke soothingly. 'I don't think you're hurt. Move your arms and legs to make sure there's nothing broken.' Janet complied and he nodded. 'Everything's all right, apparently. Come on, let's get you up on your feet.'

He slid a gentle arm around Janet's shoulders and eased her into a sitting position on the bottom stair.

'Just sit there for a moment to get over the shock.' He glanced around, saw Wenn, and rapped, 'Get some brandy, please.'

Wenn nodded and hurried into the dining-room. Sarah could see that Janet was shaking with shock. The maid's plump face was ashen, and she gazed at the suit of armour as if she could not believe what had happened.

'It could have killed me!' she gasped. 'I got the fright of my life when I looked over my shoulder and saw it toppling towards me.'

Her wide eyes looked at Sarah but did not seem to register anything at that moment, except the horror of what had happened.

'Justin was in the upper passage as I started down the stairs.' Janet spoke uncertainly. 'I told him not to get into any more mischief. He must have sneaked up behind and pushed that armour down on me. He's always tormenting the life out of me, but this time he's gone too far and something's got to be done to stop his antics. It isn't safe for a body to be around him.'

Owen made soothing noises and patted Janet's hand. Wenn returned with a glass of brandy, and Sarah went upstairs to Justin's room, frowning as she considered the implications of Janet's remarks. Elizabeth and Francis were coming along the corridor and Sarah lengthened her stride to get into Justin's room before Elizabeth could call to her.

She found Justin sitting on his bed, reading a book. He looked up briefly, a smirk on his face, and then returned his attention to the book, ignoring her presence.

'Did you not hear the disturbance on the stairs?' Sarah demanded. 'A suit of armour fell, almost hitting Janet.'

'I heard it.' Justin moistened a finger and turned a page, determined not to look up at her. 'That sort of thing usually happens to me.'

'Janet is saying you must have pushed it down on her!'

'That does not surprise me. She would say that. I get blamed for everything that happens in this house, even if it happens to me.' He did not look up from his book. 'The armour is fastened to its plinth with a rod and couldn't fall accidentally. If you think I'm strong enough to move it then think again. Why don't you ask Turner about it? I saw him upstairs. He could have overturned the suit of armour.' He resumed reading, his face impassive.

Sarah suppressed a sigh and departed, returning to the staircase, where a heated altercation was going on between Owen and Elizabeth, while Francis remained motionless beside the suit of armour. Janet and Wenn were no longer present.

Descending the staircase, Sarah paused beside the plinth where the armour usually stood and looked at the rod Justin had mentioned. One end was screwed to the wall beside the plinth — the other end had a hole bored through it to take a retaining bolt that fixed it to the suit of armour. The bolt was missing. She noticed that Francis watched her intently as she continued down the stairs.

'Of course it was Justin who did it!' Elizabeth was saying furiously. 'There's no limit to that boy's wickedness, and I've always thought he'd go too far one day. Now it's happened and no-one is safe with him around.'

Sarah thought of the urn that had apparently fallen from the roof and almost killed Justin, and it seemed to her that the boy was not the only one in the house who was not safe, but she said nothing. She paused beside Francis, who smiled at her.

'The best thing you could do is see Howard in the morning and tell him you've changed your mind about the job,' he said quietly. 'Just think, you could be miles away from here by noon.'

'That's the last thing I would consider.' Sarah smiled. 'I have a job to do here, and nothing will get in the way of that.'

Francis shrugged and moved away. He took hold of Elizabeth's arm.

'Come along,' he said forcefully. 'It's a waste of time trying to argue with Owen when he's always so right.'

'I know what I'm talking about,' Owen responded spiritedly. 'Something odd is going on in this house and I seem to be the only one who has noticed it.'

'Something odd is right,' Elizabeth responded loudly, 'and it is all down to Justin. His upbringing had been sadly neglected, and drastic measures are needed now to bring him back to normal. Far too many excuses have been made for his scandalous behaviour, and it's about time changes were made. I'd send him to boarding school.'

Francis tugged her away and they ascended the staircase, Elizabeth still muttering and fuming. Owen looked at Sarah and smiled wryly.

'I don't know what you can make of all this,' he said wearily, passing a hand across his eyes. 'Would you care for a drink? You might find that a little spirit now and again will cheer your days in the months to come. You're going to be in the thick of it whatever is going on.'

'Thank you, but I'd better go back to

Justin. Of course, he denies any knowledge of what happened to Janet. It's no wonder he acts as he does, getting the blame for everything that happens around here.'

Wenn appeared, moving soundlessly for a man of his bulk.

'Janet's feeling much better now,' he reported.

'What about this business, Wenn?' Owen demanded. He went to the suit of armour and bent over it, grasping the shoulders and exerting his strength to lift it. The armour moved slightly, and he lowered it and stood shaking his head. 'I can't believe Justin has the strength to topple this off its plinth. Anyway it's bolted in position, isn't it?'

Wenn nodded. 'It takes two of us to move it when it has to be cleaned.'

'Well, you'd better find another spot for it now.' Owen shook his head as he met Sarah's gaze. 'If it happens again someone might get seriously hurt.'

'It seems to me that everyone is in the habit of blaming Justin for these

61

incidents,' Sarah observed. 'But if he isn't guilty then who is responsible and why? And usually he is the victim, isn't he?'

'Who in his right mind would believe anything Justin said?' Owen nodded slowly. 'He said that urn fell on him but we suspect he was on the roof getting into mischief and knocked it to the ground. He must have injured himself in some other way and blamed it on the urn falling on him.'

He shrugged and went into the dining-room, emerging a moment later to cross to the library, carrying a bottle and a glass.

'Not such a good start for you, miss,' Wenn observed. 'Matters have been wrong in this house for a long time, and your arrival has corresponded with some kind of a climax. I don't know what is going on, but you'd better watch out for young Justin twenty-four hours a day, and I can't say more than that.'

Sarah frowned as she watched Wenn

return to the kitchen. She looked again at the inert suit of armour, then tested her strength on it, and was barely able to move it more than an inch or two. She shook her head decisively. Justin would not have been able to topple it off its plinth.

She went upstairs and entered Justin's room. The boy was still reading, and Sarah wondered at his lack of interest in the affair. His attitude did not seem casual. He was trying too hard to ignore what had happened. She considered for a moment, wondering how best to get him on her side.

'You couldn't possibly have pushed that suit of armour off its plinth,' she said. 'I am much stronger than you and when I attempted to lift it I couldn't move it an inch. It's much too heavy.'

Justin lowered his book immediately and looked at her, his brown eyes steady. The ghost of a smile flitted across his lips and he nodded as animation filtered into his expression. Then his impassive expression returned. He picked up the book again, and it was as if a shutter had come down between them. Sarah reached out and snatched the book from him.

'I mean it,' she said intently.

'Elizabeth thinks I did it.' Justin spoke through pinched lips. 'I tiptoed to the top of the stairs when you went down again, and heard her arguing with Owen. She's always the first to blame me for everything. She hates me.'

'I think it's a case of giving a dog a bad name,' Sarah observed. 'But it doesn't matter what is being said about you. I believe you, and you know you didn't do it, so if the armour didn't fall accidentally then the question is, who pushed it?'

Justin looked at her frowningly, and Sarah reached out and patted his shoulder.

'I can understand what you've been suffering, Justin.' She spoke softly. 'Your reaction is natural. You must be thinking the whole household is against you, but I'm here now, and if we work together we should be able to find out what is going on behind the scenes. If you accept that I am honestly trying to help you then we might make some progress. Have you any idea who is responsible?'

Justin shook his head. He gazed at Sarah as if mesmerised. His eyes glistened as unaccustomed emotion engulfed him. Then he turned and threw himself face-down on the bed and wept unrestrainedly.

Sarah gazed at his shaking body for a moment, surprised by his reaction, and then realised that the tough emotional shield he had erected against the rest of the world had been penetrated by her belief in him. She frowned, suddenly aware of how badly he had been hurt by the events attending his young life.

'I understand your feelings, Justin,' she said softly. 'But it's all over now. I'm on your side, and we'll beat this thing, whatever it is. Why don't you get into bed and sleep?'

Justin nodded, keeping his face

averted, and Sarah left him. She paced her own room, uneasy with conflicting thoughts. Her mind was agonising over what she had learned.

The only thing of importance that came to her was the fact that she could not relax for a minute. Watching Justin to ensure his safety would occupy her time and effort twenty-four hours a day.

She went to bed with that grim thought in mind and, after a timeless period of tossing and turning, slept uneasily through the seemingly unending night. Awakening early next morning, she found that the situation had not lessened in her mind, her fears for Justin's safety being even sharper than the night before.

By the time she was ready to face the day she was attracted to Justin's room by the sound of voices, and opened the connecting door to find Janet placing a large breakfast tray on the small table by the window. Justin was fully dressed and looking very alert as Janet laid the table with the breakfast, rattling crockery and cutlery with perverse enthusiasm. The maid looked round when Sarah entered the room.

'How are you feeling this morning, Janet?' Sarah enquired.

'Very well, thank you.' Janet bestowed a hard look at Justin. 'My nerves are unsteady, but my ankle is all right if I don't put too much weight on it. I'm going to see Mr Howard this morning. I can't continue to work here under the present routine. It's more than my life is worth to keep ignoring all the accidents that happen.'

'I'm sorry to hear that.' Sarah glanced at Justin. He was seating himself at the table, apparently not listening to their conversation, but he perked up and looked at Sarah when she continued. 'Janet, I hope you're not still under the impression that Justin had something to do with that suit of armour falling down the stairs. I couldn't move that armour unaided, and neither could Owen. Wenn said it always takes two men to shift it at cleaning time. So get it straight in your mind that Justin is not guilty.'

'If you say so.' Janet sniffed. 'You will be having your breakfast here with Justin. The other tutors did. You'd better eat now. The food is not very hot. It has to come all the way from the kitchen, and porridge soon turns cold.'

Sarah moved to the table as Janet picked up her tray and prepared to depart.

'Wait a moment,' Sarah said firmly, and the maid paused uncertainly. 'Why does Justin have his breakfast up here?'

'Them's Miss Elizabeth's orders.' A sulky note crept into Janet's voice. 'Master Howard doesn't eat breakfast in the dining-room, and Justin isn't allowed in there with the rest of the family unless the master is present.'

'Justin is not an animal.' Anger edged Sarah's voice. 'That porridge is already too cold to eat, and look at the brown skin congealing on it. Justin may be accustomed to eating his food in that state but I am not. Take it back to the kitchen and we'll have fresh porridge served in the dining-room.'

A faint smile flitted across Janet's face as she refilled her tray. Then she departed, muttering under her breath. Sarah looked at Justin, saw a smile on his lips, and nodded decisively.

'If you're not careful you'll set Elizabeth against you, and then you might have accidents happening to you,' Justin observed.

'Let me worry about that. Come on, let's go down to the dining-room and assert our rights.'

Sarah had a few misgivings when Justin opened the door of the dining-room and she entered. He followed her closely, without the customary slamming of the heavy door, and Sarah approached the table, where Elizabeth and Francis were seated opposite Owen and Adam at the nearer end of the long table.

The chatter that had been going had cut off when the door opened, and a somewhat shocked silence ensued. Elizabeth's face showed that she could not believe her eyes, and her mouth opened and closed like a fish out of water as she tried to overcome her surprise. Owen glared at them with narrowed gaze. His lips were pinched. Adam nodded and smiled faintly, while Francis shook his head in disapproval.

5

'What is the meaning of this?' Elizabeth demanded. 'Were you not told it's an inflexible rule that we are spared the torment of Justin's presence at breakfast? Remove Justin at once and Janet will serve his breakfast in his room as usual.'

'I won't do that.' Sarah spoke firmly. 'I have never heard anything so ridiculous! Janet served breakfast in Justin's room, and I was appalled. The porridge was cold. Your decision to bar Justin from the dining-room is tantamount to cruelty. I have Howard's full authority to act as I see fit in all matters pertaining to Justin's welfare. We will not leave. We shall sit at the other end of the table to eat like civilised human beings.'

Silence followed Sarah's words. Owen was gaping in shock and so was

Elizabeth, while Francis sat back in his chair with a half-smile on his smooth face. Adam grinned and nodded, then got to his feet and came around the table to Sarah's side.

'Well said,' he declared. 'Elizabeth has had her way far too long. It's about time she was put in her place, and you're in need of support from the family. I agree with your decision. Come and sit at the other end of the table and I'll join you. Come along, Justin. Take Grandfather's seat, as it will be yours one day.'

Sarah was relieved by Adam's reaction, and allowed herself to be led to the top end of the table. Justin seated himself in Howard's sacred place and Sarah sat on his right. Adam fetched his plate from where he had been sitting and sat down opposite Sarah, an amused grin on his handsome face.

'Truth to tell, I've been uneasy about the enmity Justin has faced in the family,' Adam remarked.

Sarah glanced at Justin and saw that

he was pleasantly surprised by Adam's words. She saw Elizabeth get to her feet to storm out of the dining-room, followed by a resigned Francis, but Elizabeth met Wenn in the doorway and paused to voice her feelings further.

'Wenn, in future I shall be eating my breakfast in the library,' she declared.

Wenn approached the top end of the table, his expression professionally bland.

'Janet has informed me of the change in Master Justin's breakfast routine,' he said gravely. 'Fresh porridge is being prepared, and will be served shortly.'

'Thank you.' Sarah forced herself to relax. She smiled at Justin, who was watching her with a glint of amusement in his brown eyes.

'Pay no heed to Elizabeth's protests.' Adam was apparently amused by his sister's violent reaction. 'Her problem is that she blames Justin for her return from Cornwall. She has always insisted that it is her duty to supervise his upbringing, despite the fact that

Howard is adamant she is not needed, yet she has never concerned herself over much with Justin.'

'I'm greatly concerned about Justin,' Sarah replied, 'and I've started as I mean to go on.' She glanced at her wristwatch. 'I have to see Howard at eight-thirty, and I'll confirm my position on handling Justin.'

Adam looked at Justin, who was toying with the cutlery before him.

'What are your plans for today? Do you start lessons this morning?'

Justin shook his head, deciding not to voice a reply, and Sarah stepped into the breach.

'We are not doing lessons this first week,' she said. 'Justin needs to relax before I start plying him with education. Can you suggest suitable places of interest in the locality where I could take him?'

'I can do better than that.' Adam paused as Janet approached with breakfast for Sarah and Justin, and continued when the maid had departed. 'If I may, I'll accompany you and renew my acquaintance with Justin in the process.'

'But aren't you too busy running the estate?' Sarah enquired.

'I have been in the past, but it's time I thought of myself. I am a member of the family and not some faithful retainer to be ground down by daily routine.' Adam stood up. 'I think a trip to Shepton will suffice for your first outing.'

Sarah turned her attention to Justin, who was eating stolidly.

'Would you like us to go with Adam today?'

Justin shrugged as he spooned porridge into his mouth. He glanced at Adam, who was waiting for his reply, and appeared to like the unaccustomed attention he was receiving. He paused for a moment, then nodded, and Adam smiled and departed.

Owen finished his breakfast and arose to move into the seat Adam had vacated. His pale face was taut and his eyes gleamed with excitement as he looked at Sarah's impassive features.

'You've really done it now,' he said. 'Elizabeth never loses a fight.'

Sarah glanced at her watch.

'I shall be seeing Howard shortly, but he won't take Elizabeth's part. I have firm instructions on what to do, and Justin's welfare is of prime importance.'

'Why has Adam allied himself to your cause?' Owen shook his head. 'He's wasted no time picking his side, but then I always thought Adam knew which side of his bread was buttered.'

'Adam is going out with us this morning,' Justin said.

Owen's jaw dropped in amazement. Then he laughed and said, 'I didn't know you had a sense of humour, Justin. Well done.'

'It's true!' Justin's expression turned sulky at Owen's obvious disbelief, and Sarah reached out and squeezed the boy's shoulder, warning him to be quiet. Justin subsided into his habitual impassiveness.

Owen arose. 'I'm planning to go into

Shepton this morning,' he mused, 'and I'll be using the car. Turner doubles as chauffeur, and if you're going into town then it would be better if we travelled together to save Turner an extra trip. What time are you leaving?'

'We haven't decided yet, and I shall prefer to be alone with Justin on this first day.' Sarah met Justin's eyes as the boy looked up at her, and shook her head slightly.

Relief showed on Justin's face.

'I don't want to go with you, Owen,' he said firmly, following Sarah's line. 'We are supposed to be on holiday this week, and you don't know how to have fun.'

Owen scowled. 'I don't suppose I could endure your tantrums and tricks,' he observed sourly, and departed.

'Time to talk to Howard,' Sarah said, glancing at her watch. 'You can sit here quite comfortably and finish your breakfast. We've established your right to be here but behave yourself and, when you've finished, please go back to your room and wait for me there.'

He nodded, spreading marmalade on a piece of toast.

'You are better than all my other tutors put together,' he observed, 'and if Grandfather has given you the right to do as you please then we can give Elizabeth a good run for her money.'

'That's not what it is all about,' Sarah said firmly, 'so please don't take that attitude.'

She left Justin at the table, made her way to Howard's study, and checked her watch as she tapped at the door. The time was exactly eight-thirty, and she was a little surprised when Howard bade her enter.

She opened the door, half-expecting Elizabeth to be inside, in full flow with a complaint about her, but Howard was alone, seated in an easy-chair before the fire. He looked weary, as if he had not slept well during the night.

Howard motioned her to a seat.

'I have already had a report on your progress. Elizabeth was waiting for me when I came down. I had a feeling she would turn out to be your main hurdle and she hasn't disappointed me. I heard what she had to say, then explained that she had no authority to oppose you on any matter pertaining to Justin's welfare. She didn't like that and proclaimed her intention of returning to Cornwall forthwith.'

'I had no wish to upset anyone,' Sarah replied.

'Don't worry.' He chuckled. 'Elizabeth has made that selfsame threat several times but so far she has not stirred in that direction. It will do the family good to meet some opposition to their present way of life. Justin is the only one who matters in this and I'm sure you will be good for him.'

'He's already behaving himself very well. I think he's regarding me as a friend. I'm taking him into Shepton for the day and Adam has offered to accompany us.'

'Adam? Did you accept his offer?'

'Yes, I did. It seemed to be what Justin wanted.'

'This is even better than I hoped for. Do what you can to encourage Adam to take some time off from his estate duties. He drives himself far too hard. I've been trying to get him to take a holiday but he always says he cannot find the time.

'I suspect his intention to overwork is based on his unfortunate affair with Agatha French, and it is high time he recovered from that nonsense, but Adam is very sensitive and his disappointment must have hit him hard. That is neither here nor there, however. What happened to Janet last night?'

Sarah explained the incident and Howard shook his head.

'I agree that Justin could not have pushed the armour off its plinth, and it certainly did not fall accidentally.'

'The bolt is missing from the retaining rod and cannot be found anywhere. It does look as if someone removed it deliberately, but why would the armour be pushed over when Janet was descending the stairs? If someone was out to harm Justin surely they would have waited for him to be on the stairs instead of Janet.'

Howard nodded. 'That thought had crossed my mind, but more to the point is who wants harm to come to Justin, and why? It can't be on account of his bad behaviour, so is it the boy's inheritance? It seems it is not just harm being planned, but Justin's death, if the incident of the urn falling from the roof is anything to go by. Justin would most certainly have been killed had it caught him squarely.

'If someone is out to kill my great-grandson then we have an awful duty to perform. But who in my family would contemplate such a desperate step? If the motive is Justin's inherit-ance then Adam is most likely to be involved, for he would inherit on Justin's death.'

Thinking of her first impressions of the family, Sarah felt a protest arise in her mind at Howard's words.

'I don't think that is the case,' she replied. 'I have an intuitive feeling that Adam is not to blame.'

'Can you make out a similar case for Owen? And Elizabeth? She is making the most fuss about your presence here. There is a saying about not trusting Greeks bearing gifts, and Adam has extended the hand of friendship to you. Examine his motives very carefully, Sarah, before accepting him at face value.'

There was a knock at the door and Elizabeth entered.

'Sorry,' she said. 'I didn't know you were busy. I'm off to Shepton now, Grandfather. Francis is not going with me. He decided at the last moment that his art is more important than a day out with me.'

She withdrew immediately, and Howard shook his head.

'They are drawing up sides,' he mused. 'Be careful, Sarah. It's not so much a question of who is your enemy, but who are your friends? I'm afraid I cannot advise you with any certainty. All of this is beyond me.'

Sarah went back to the dining-room but Justin was not there so she hurried up the staircase, and paused when she saw the suit of armour back on its plinth.

Frowning, she inspected it closely, and sighed with relief when she saw that a fresh bolt and a padlock had been fitted to the retaining rod. She went on to Justin's room, and was surprised to discover that he was not there.

Janet was ascending the staircase when Sarah descended in search of Justin and they met on the landing. Janet's face was showing the haggard result of the shock she had received the evening before, and Sarah paused and reached out to touch the maid's shoulder.

'How are you feeling, Janet?' she enquired.

'I'm all right, miss, and I don't blame

Justin for what happened. I'm sure now that he couldn't have done it. I hope your influence will calm him down but I'm not surprised he acts like he does, the way he's been treated.'

'Have you seen him recently. I told him to go to his room when he finished breakfast and now I can't find him.'

Janet smiled wanly. 'That's Justin for you — never a dull moment. I haven't seen him since I served breakfast in the dining-room, but then he's always missing when someone wants him. Why don't you check with Wenn? He seems to know everything that goes on in this house, him and that old crow he calls his wife.'

Sarah frowned as she went down to the kitchen, wondering at the undercurrents of life in the manor. She found Wenn and Matilda sitting at the large table, drinking tea, and Wenn was reading a newspaper. The butler sprang up at her entrance but the housekeeper remained impassive, her shoe-button eyes regarding Sarah intently.

'Have you seen Justin in the last five minutes?' Sarah enquired.

'No, miss. He was in the dining-room when I saw him last,' Wenn replied. 'I'll have a scout round and see if I can locate him.'

'Don't worry. I don't want to raise a hue and cry for him. I'm sure I shall find him.'

Sarah departed hurriedly, aware of the intensity of Matilda's gaze, and almost bumped into Owen as he emerged from the library when she entered.

'Have you seen Justin?' she enquired.

'I was about to come for you,' Owen replied. 'I saw Justin enter here a few minutes ago and feared he was up to no good so I followed him. He's gone into the priest-hole, and I put the catch on the panel to keep him in there. Come on, I'll show you.'

Sarah frowned as she entered the library and followed Owen to the secret panel. Owen showed her the catch that unlocked the panel, and then operated the mechanism. The panel slid open and Owen uttered a little cry of shock. Sarah crowded forward to look into the cell-like secret room, which was empty. If Justin had been locked in the priest-hole then he must have vanished into thin air.

6

'I don't believe this,' Owen said. 'Where on earth has he got to? I locked him in here and there's no way he could have got out with the catch on, unless there's another panel that I don't know about.'

He entered the secret room and began searching the bare walls. Sarah watched him intently, shaking her head. Her thoughts were troubled. She caught sight of a furtive movement in the library from a corner of her eye and turned swiftly to see Justin coming towards her from the window overlooking the terrace.

He put a finger to his lips and came to her side to look into the priest-hole, then reached out and pressed the mechanism. Sarah protested as the panel slid smoothly into place, cutting off a cry of alarm from Owen. Justin pressed the protuberance that locked the panel.

'Let's leave Owen in there all day,' he said.

'We couldn't possibly do that.' Sarah was shocked by his callousness. 'How did you get out of the priest-hole when Owen locked it?'

'There's another room behind the first.' Justin grinned. 'In olden days, if searchers found the first room empty, they wouldn't think of looking for a second one and the priest would be safe. Owen only knows about the first one. The second one has a short tunnel connecting it to a panel by the grandfather clock. The tunnel leads to an exit in the outside wall so it's possible to escape without coming back into this room.'

'How did you learn about all these secret places?'

'Grandfather showed me because I'll inherit the manor when he dies.'

Justin reached out again and opened the panel. Owen emerged, looking irate.

'How did you get out?' Owen demanded. 'I locked you in.'

Justin shook his head.

'There are some things you are not meant to know,' he replied.

'Why did you come in here and hide?' Sarah asked. 'I told you to go up to your room when you finished breakfast.'

Justin shrugged, and would say nothing further despite prompting from Sarah. Owen shook his head in frustration, then departed, and Justin sniggered as his uncle left the library.

'You shouldn't plague Owen like that,' Sarah reproved. 'You need to make a friend of him. It would be better for you in the long run.'

'Why should I? Owen doesn't like me because I stand between him and this place. He might be the one trying to kill me.'

Sarah was horrified. 'Don't say things like that!' she implored.

'Even if it's true?' His eyes glinted. 'I am alone in this, you know. Grandfather is too old to do anything, and everyone else would be pleased to see the back of me. Even the servants feel that way. I've seen it in their faces.'

'Surely you don't believe that.'

'I do.' Justin was adamant. 'I've seen the way they look at me. The servants wish something bad would happen to me.'

'That's because your behaviour has been so atrocious, but Adam is on your side. He's even offered to spend a day with us in Shepton.'

Justin shook his head stubbornly.

'It's you he's interested in, not me. He's liked all the lady tutors I've had.' He looked at her guilelessly, his dark eyes glistening, and Sarah reached out and ruffled his hair playfully.

'Go on with you,' she reproved lightly. 'If we're late, Adam may have another thought about going to Shepton.'

'He won't miss the opportunity of being in your company,' Justin replied.

Shortly before ten o'clock, Sarah and Justin went down to the hall to find

Adam there, talking to Howard. They both seemed unusually grim, but their expressions lightened when they heard Justin's approach and turned to greet the boy. Adam nodded at something Howard was saying, and the older man smiled rather grimly as he met Sarah's gaze.

'Are we going into Shepton?' Justin demanded.

'Certainly, unless Sarah has decided on some other place.'

Adam was wearing a light blue suit and seemed to be a different person in manner, as if he had discarded his estate worries along with his working suit of velveteen trousers and tweed jacket. He smiled at Sarah, but she noticed that his friendliness, which marked her first impressions of him, had receded, as if he had been warned to keep his distance.

The thought struck her like a flash of lightning, and she subjected Howard to a searching glance, for no-one else in the household could give such a warning to a man like Adam. She suppressed a sigh, for Howard did not seem authoritative at all, his expression merely showing uneasiness.

'Justin is keen on Shepton, and I've never been there,' Sarah replied in answer to Adam's question, aware that a cold spot had suddenly made its home in her heart.

'Justin seems like a different boy this morning,' Howard observed in an aside to Sarah. 'You must be good for him, but remember not to let him out of your sight for an instant.' He raised his voice. 'Go and enjoy yourself, Justin. It's been nothing but doom and gloom for you these past months. Here's some money to spend.' He held out some notes encircled by an elastic band, and Justin took the money eagerly, rifling through it excitedly.

'Thank you, Grandad.' Justin's dark eyes were beaming.

Howard smiled and turned away to return to his study. Adam moved towards the front door, where Wenn was waiting patiently to open it for them.

'We'll use my car,' Adam said. 'Turner has taken Elizabeth and Owen to Shepton in the big car.'

Adam ushered them out to the terrace, and Sarah looked at the autumn landscape. She was looking forward to the day's outing despite her feelings, and gazed around with interest as they descended the terrace steps to where a smart red and black roadster was waiting.

'One day I want a car like this,' Justin observed as he climbed into the back.

'One day you'll be able to buy whatever you like,' Adam responded, and Sarah glanced quickly at him, but saw nothing significant in his expression.

'Do you love going out in a car?' Justin demanded, leaning across the back of Sarah's seat to speak to her. He was excited now by the prospect of a day out. 'It's wonderful.'

Sarah glanced at Justin and smiled.

He was acting like a normal child now, and she could imagine the dreary life he had been leading, but that was in the past, she vowed, and in future there would be no worries for him.

Sarah relaxed to enjoy the drive but found her gaze being drawn time and again to Adam's profile. He was concentrating on his driving and she was able to look at him with impunity. He had a strong chin and looked very handsome, with the kind of looks that appealed to her, but despite the easy smile on his lips he seemed to be preoccupied with an underlying seriousness.

All too soon the small car was gliding down a long decline to enter the main street of Shepton, a small market town nestling in a fold in the moors. Adam parked the car in a private road leading to the vicarage and church, and they alighted. Sarah reached out and grasped Justin's shoulder as the boy made as if to dart off in his excitement, and he looked up at her, his eyes shining. He was hugely elated, but made an effort to contain his feelings.

'I have an understanding with Reverend Jennings about parking,' Adam said. 'An annual donation to the church fund takes care of it.' He gave his attention to Justin. 'Now, let's make a really good day of this. It's your treat so what would you like to do first?'

'Shopping,' Justin replied without hesitation, 'to buy a chemistry set.'

They visited the shops, and Sarah remained in the background, watching points as Adam and Justin pursued Justin's intention to buy a chemistry set. When they finally selected a set it proved to be much more expensive than Justin could afford, and Adam paid the extra money without demur.

Justin was bright-eyed and cheerful when they left the shop. He was clutching his purchase as if afraid that it might suddenly disappear, and was reluctant to hand it over when Adam suggested taking it back to the car.

'Sarah will take you into that restaurant along the street while I put the package in the car,' Adam said. 'You don't need to be cluttered up with such a large item. I'll be back shortly, and after refreshments we'll visit the museum.' He took the chemistry set.

'There isn't much to do in a place like this,' Justin grumbled. 'The town is too small to be worth a long visit.'

'It could be worse,' Sarah reminded. 'We might have started lessons today.'

'Whose idea was it to start with a holiday?' Justin gazed after Adam's tall figure.

'It was a mutual decision because it seemed a good way for us to become acquainted.'

'I'm glad you came. You seem different from my other tutors.' Justin started along the street to the restaurant. 'Can I have a sticky bun?'

'You can have anything you desire,' Sarah told him.

Justin stopped short when they

entered the restaurant, and Sarah, looking in the direction of his gaze, saw Elizabeth Fernley seated at a table with a woman.

'I don't want to talk to Aunt Elizabeth,' Justin said doggedly. 'Just seeing her spoils everything. Do you think she's come to spy on us?'

'That's hardly likely.' Sarah led him to a corner well away from his aunt's table, aware that the woman had observed their entrance but gave no sign of awareness beyond a narrowed glance.

Adam appeared, and seemed taken aback by the sight of his sister, but merely lifted a hand in acknowledgement and came to sit down opposite Sarah. He smiled, a superficial gesture, and Sarah wondered if he was concerned about causing trouble between the family and himself for taking her side, but he chatted normally and Sarah relaxed.

7

Sarah spent the rest of the day in Justin's company, unable to think naturally because her mind seemed to have set off at a tangent, trying to concentrate on the gigantic task of safeguarding the boy at all times. She was remotely aware that Adam was disturbing her with his presence, looming large on the periphery of her mind.

Justin was engrossed with his new chemistry set until bedtime, taxing Sarah's scant knowledge of the subject to its limit until Adam joined them in the library, volunteering the information that chemistry had been one of his favourite subjects at school. It was then that they began to make progress with the basic experiments outlined in the set, and Sarah was content to sit back and watch with interest, her thoughts turning to Adam and questioning his motives for the sudden interest he was showing in Justin.

Did he have an ulterior motive? Upon her arrival she had somehow gained the impression that Adam was above guilt, but realised that her judgement might have been clouded by relief at the way he had rescued her from the predicament of being lost in the darkness.

Justin was reluctant to call it a day when she finally said it was time he went to bed, but Adam backed her decision and the chemistry set was put away. Adam remained in the library when Sarah escorted Justin to his bedroom. She was amazed that the boy's manner had changed so much in one short day, but realised that his interest had been engaged, and it was possible that he would not revert to his previous anti-social ways.

He prepared for bed without objection. Sarah locked the door of his room on the inside before leaving him, explaining her decision to do so and advising him that she would not be far away in her own room.

'I've always wanted my door locked.' Justin spoke thoughtfully. 'I sometimes hear noises in the corridor, and I'm sure someone rattles my door handle to frighten me because the noise makes me think the house is haunted.'

Sarah went back to the library to find Adam in a reflective mood. He was looking at a book he had taken from one of the shelves, but replaced the tome and faced her, his incisive gaze studying her face in a way that disconcerted her.

'I have given a lot of thought to the situation that seems to exist here,' he said. 'Your job is to teach Justin, but you cannot be expected to do anything more than that. However, I think you're going to have to watch points very closely, even if it makes your job more difficult.'

'Do you think Justin's life is in danger?'

Her tone was natural although fear spread quickly through her and she fought to maintain a grip on her nerve.

'I don't know what to think right now.' His brow was furrowed, his eyes filled with calculation. 'On the face of it there's nothing to point us in any particular direction, but if Justin is telling the truth about the accidents that have happened to him then the situation could be most serious.'

'If someone is guilty of trying to harm him, whom do you suppose it is? Can it be someone outside your immediate family circle?' Sarah asked.

Adam gazed at her steadily for a moment, then shook his head and sighed heavily.

'The alternative is too shocking to contemplate,' he said. 'Actually, I'm one step ahead of you because you don't know if you can trust me, but I know I wouldn't hurt a hair of Justin's head. So who would benefit from his death? I'm next in line to inherit if Justin died, and I would have to die, too, for Owen to benefit. There's Elizabeth, who would have to see out Owen and myself after killing Justin.'

'For the record, I have to suspect your motives, and Owen's, because I don't know either of you. I suppose all we can do is watch and wait to see what develops, but it will make my job very difficult.'

'I agree but everything pales beside the thought that something bad might happen to the boy and we cannot afford to take that chance. In future I'll do what I can to ease your job. I'll be watching the situation as best I can. I must say that Justin is lucky to have someone like you watching over him. I was watching you today most critically, and couldn't fault you anywhere. Apart from that, I enjoyed myself also, and I hope we can combine watching out for Justin with more such days out.'

'Thank you.' Sarah smiled. 'I shall try to get Justin away from the house as much as possible.'

Adam looked relieved as he moved away.

'I will see you in the morning, when we'll talk about another excursion. I have to go now because there are still some jobs to be done before I can call it a day. Thank you again for such a good time. Good-night, Sarah.'

'Good-night.' She sighed as he departed, her thoughts turning upon him. Although her intuition informed her that he could not be responsible for Justin's problems, there was still a doubt in her mind.

She examined the books in the library until she decided to go to bed, and the big house seemed deathly silent and still as she made her way up to her room. She had to fight an impulse to glance over her shoulder when she reached the upper corridors for the shadows were eerie, and she could understand why Justin had a thing about sleeping with the door of his room locked.

She was about to enter her room

when footsteps sounded on the uncarpeted floor, causing her to look round quickly. A tall figure was coming from the rear of the house, and a sigh gusted from her when she recognised Frank Turner.

The footman was checking the doors of the unoccupied rooms, and waved to her. She returned the acknowledgement and entered her room, not wanting to talk, but he caught up with her before she could close the door.

'Had a good day? I saw you in Shepton.'

'I enjoyed it very much,' she responded.

'When do you get a day off? I could show you a good time if we can arrange the same day off duty.'

His brown eyes carried a glint that made Sarah feel uneasy.

'Thank you, but I don't think I shall be taking many days off to start with.'

'Don't let them overwork you. They're good at that. Don't be taken in by their apparent friendliness either. They'd use you for their own ends then drop you without a second thought.'

'I shall do the job I came for, and expect nothing more,' Sarah replied. 'Good-night.'

She entered the room and closed the door, half-fearing that he might hinder her in some way, such was her impression, but she heard his departing footsteps and turned the key in the lock.

When she finally got into bed she had difficulty sleeping immediately because her wearisome thoughts were going round and round in her head, but eventually tiredness won the battle against her consciousness and she slept uneasily until noises in Justin's room awakened her.

Checking her watch, she saw the time was seven-thirty, and arose to start the new day, her natural optimism colouring her thoughts.

'What are we going to do today?' Justin demanded the instant she looked into his room. He was dressed and looked quite presentable.

Sarah smiled. 'What would you like to do?'

'I don't want to return to Shepton so perhaps I could show you round the estate this morning. Later, we could get out the chemistry set and try some more experiments.'

'Would you like to stay in all day and use the chemistry set?'

'I would, but I know you wouldn't agree to that,' Justin laughed. 'I'll settle for doing what you think I ought to do this morning if we can spend the afternoon doing what I want.'

'That's fair, but we'd better not make a decision now because Adam will talk to us at breakfast and he may have a different idea of what to do.'

'I hope we're not going to have him hanging around all the time. I don't mind, but he's not interested in me, and he should keep his interest in you for when you're off duty.'

'I shall see to it that he doesn't monopolise my time,' Sarah told him. 'It seems to me that Adam is in need of help, and we need him as an ally in this business that's going on around you.' She suppressed a shiver as she looked at his cheerful face. He seemed so young and innocent, and it was difficult to accept that someone might be trying to harm him. 'So let us help Adam by having him along with us whenever we can and he may save us some grief if matters get worse.

'Let's go to breakfast.' Sarah placed a hand on his shoulder as they went down to the dining-room.

Justin opened the door for her and Sarah entered to face a barrage of gazes. She was surprised to see Elizabeth present after the incident of the morning before. The woman nodded an acknowledgement. She was seated beside Francis, who smiled sheepishly when Sarah met his gaze. Owen was sitting slumped in his customary seat, but Adam was not yet present.

'Good morning.'

Sarah spoke generally and Francis answered civilly. Elizabeth's lips moved in response but no sound issued from her mouth. Owen merely looked up and nodded gloomily. No-one spoke to Justin. He stayed on Sarah's right as they went to the top of the table, as if using her as a shield.

Sarah seated Justin at the head of the table and then went to the sideboard to get their meal. As they ate, she discovered that she was keen to see Adam, but he had not appeared by the time they finished breakfast. Elizabeth and Francis departed quickly, and it was obvious that they had come to the dining-room earlier than usual. Owen finished his meal and came to speak to Sarah.

'You haven't made a friend of Elizabeth.' Owen sat down opposite Sarah and leaned forward to put his elbows on the table.

'Does it really matter?' Sarah countered. 'It was just a storm in a tea cup.'

'Elizabeth doesn't think so.' Owen got to his feet. 'What are you two doing today?'

'We haven't decided yet.' Sarah pushed aside her plate.

Justin had finished his meal and was waiting patiently for her.

'I shall be showing Sarah round the estate this morning,' he said sharply to forestall an invitation from Owen. 'Do you know anything about chemistry, Owen?'

Owen frowned at the unexpected question, and thrust out his underlip.

'I did some chemistry at school but never liked it. I didn't think I would ever need it in later life so I never bothered about it. Why do you ask?'

Justin shrugged and Owen departed. Wenn entered the room followed by Turner, who began to clear the sideboard. Wenn approached Sarah.

'Everything all right this morning, miss?' he enquired.

'Yes, thank you. Has Adam been in for breakfast yet?'

'He had an early breakfast, miss. The vet was summoned before dawn to attend one of the mares, and Master

109

Adam likes to be present at the examination.'

Justin arose and Sarah did likewise.

'May I ask what your plans are for today?' Wenn asked.

'We haven't made any yet,' Sarah replied.

Wenn nodded and went about his duties. Sarah felt slightly disappointed that Adam had not appeared at breakfast, but she realised that estate duties would always come first with him, which was as it should be . . .

They went out for a walk, and although Sarah watched for Adam he did not show up. They spent the morning looking around the estate, went into the house for lunch, and still Adam did not put in an appearance.

It was not until evening, when they were in the library, that Adam appeared, and he seemed tired and ill at ease. When Sarah questioned him about the health of the estate horses he made no particular reply, and left soon afterwards, pleading pressure of work.

Sarah felt crushed by his distant manner after the friendliness he had displayed in Shepton the day before, and she agonised over the situation when she went to bed that night.

Several days passed without incident, and Adam hardly put in an appearance during that time. Sarah took Justin out on daily excursions, but the boy seemed interested in nothing but his chemistry set, and although he showed some feeling for the places they visited he was always keen to get back to the manor.

On Sunday, a week after her arrival and the day before Justin was due to begin lessons, Sarah decided that they should visit the local church, and Justin agreed, although his face showed reluctance.

'I'll show you a shortcut to the church through the estate. If we go round by the road it will take thirty minutes to walk there. The others go to church in the car, but they don't like me to travel with them. They sit in the family pew in the very front of the congregation, but I have to sit at the back because I'm so troublesome,' Justin declared.

Sarah nodded. 'I can insist on you sitting up front if you wish,' she observed.

'No, thank you.' Justin shuddered in mock horror. 'It would be terrible having to sit next to the one who is trying to kill me.'

Sarah, sobered by his words, was thoughtful when they went to their rooms to prepare for their visit to the church.

A chill wind blew into their faces when they ventured outside, and a sudden spattering of rain rattled against the window panes. Sarah turned up the collar of her coat and grasped Justin by the shoulder as he turned to hurry back into the house.

'It's a perfect morning for walking, Justin.' She spoke firmly. 'We are going to church.'

'We shall get wet,' Justin protested.

'Nonsense!' She glanced at the group

of single-storey stable buildings half-hidden by tall poplars that were swaying in the strong breeze and wondered about Adam. Was he truly kept so busy by his estate duties or was he deliberately avoiding her?

Justin glanced up at her and seemed to read her thoughts.

'I wonder what's going on at the stables,' he mused. 'We'd better not go over there to see if Adam is going to church because he never does. He's had the vet in every day this week, looking at one of the horses. I'll show you my favourite spot on the way to the church. The day is wild enough for the river to be exciting. Instead of going to church, we could go out in one of the boats at the boathouse. Come on.'

Sarah followed Justin as he started along a narrow path that led away from the house. They passed under a clump of trees and emerged on the river bank. Sarah paused to survey the scene.

In the foreground was an ivy-covered boathouse with a small wooden jetty in front of it. An assortment of small craft were moored to the staging, all bobbing and jerking at their mooring ropes as wind and water tugged and chivvied them.

'We won't even contemplate using a boat this morning.' Sarah gazed in consternation at the swiftly-flowing river that was barely contained between its grassy banks. 'I'm a strong swimmer, but I wouldn't like to take my chances in that current. Is the river always that high?'

Justin shook his head.

'We've had a lot of rain lately, and there's a lot more to come. I want to show you my favourite spot.'

'There's something out there now, being swept downstream by the current,' Sarah observed, and pointed to the middle of the river, where the current was really fast-flowing.

Justin looked and shook his head.

'It's a tree trunk. There's a stack of them on the low pasture upstream across the river, and it looks as if the water has got to them. Those that get swept away usually finish jammed up at the bend about a mile down-river.'

He hurried on to the right, passing behind the boathouse, and Sarah followed closely until they came to a wide stream that entered the river at a right-angle. A narrow wooden bridge with safety rails spanned the stream where it entered the river.

Justin hurried onto the bridge and leaned on the rail to look down into the river. Sarah called a warning for him to be careful, then gasped in horror as the rail swung outwards under his weight, carrying him off the bridge and over the river.

8

Sarah gazed transfixed at the spot where Justin had disappeared, her mind numbed with shock, but before she realised what she was doing she had flung off her coat and kicked off her shoes.

Justin's head reappeared above the surface at that moment, one arm upflung as he struggled desperately to stay afloat in the tumultuous water. Sarah ran several yards to the left, for Justin was being carried along rapidly towards the boathouse.

She dived into the river in a low arc. The shock of the cold water was appalling. She surfaced, gasping, and saw that her momentum had carried her almost within an arm's length of Justin. She propelled herself towards him, striking out furiously, and grasped his uplifted arm as he sank again.

Kicking out powerfully, she brought his head above the surface and turned him, warning him not to struggle, her mouth close to his ear. She looked around to see that they were being carried towards the boathouse and the jetty.

The five small boats at the landing stage were moored bows to stern and formed a barrier as they were swept inexorably towards them. Sarah realised that the boats were their only chance of survival. She twisted until her back was towards them, and gripped Justin with her left arm under his armpit and across his chest, holding him firmly.

The next instant she was thrown against the nearest boat with a force that almost knocked the breath from her lungs. The current tried to drag them around the boat but Sarah reached out with her right hand, grasped the boat and anchored them against it while the current clawed at them like a thousand sea-devils trying to tear them loose.

Justin reached up and secured a one-handed hold on the boat. Sarah grasped his other hand and pushed it onto the boat. He closed his fingers on the slippery woodwork and dragged himself upwards while Sarah thrust at him from below. She kicked with her legs and almost threw him into the boat, but the power she used forced her under the surface. She was gripped by the current and dragged under the rowing boat.

She surfaced on the other side of the boat, spluttering and gasping for air, chilled by the cold water, and was struck a heavy blow by one of the uprights of the jetty, which stopped her headlong movement with the current.

She clutched at the slippery wood-work but her strength had been sapped by her efforts and she could do nothing more to save herself. She gasped for breath as she tried to wedge herself against the jetty, but the all-powerful current broke her frantic grip and began to sweep her out into open water, wherein lay disaster.

Then a powerful hand came down from the landing stage and seized her left arm at the elbow. She was plucked from the water and deposited upon the landing stage, where she lay gasping for breath, utterly spent. Adam's voice sounded in her ears — the sweetest thing she had ever heard.

'Justin!' Sarah gasped, her teeth chattering uncontrollably.

'He's all right. I saw what happened. I spotted you passing the stable and came to warn you to be careful down here. Just a minute and I'll get him out of the boat.'

Adam jumped into one of the boats and lifted Justin from it, then stepped on to the jetty with the boy's limp figure in his arms. Sarah felt a surge of fear in her breast. Had Justin drowned despite her efforts?

Justin appeared to be all right. He was wide-eyed in shock, but managed to grin wanly at her, reaching out to clutch at her hand in appreciation of her efforts to save him.

'We'd better get you both back to the house,' Adam remarked. 'Explanations can wait. I saw what happened as I came towards the river, but I don't understand why.'

'The rail gave way when I put my weight on it,' Justin said. He was shivering convulsively. 'It was loose. I've leaned on it a hundred times before and it never moved.'

Sarah smiled in relief for the sound of Justin's voice broke through the mental fog that seemed to encompass her brain. She slipped her arm through Adam's as they hurried towards the house.

'Sarah saved me!' Justin spoke in a high-pitched tone, and Sarah heard his teeth chattering. 'That rail gave way, Adam. It broke. Another of those accidents that keep happening to me. Sarah pushed me into the boat. I couldn't get out of the water by myself.'

'Don't talk about it now,' Adam said. He glanced sideways at Sarah, and there was such an expression of relief on his face that she almost choked on the emotion that arose in her breast.

'Are you all right?' he asked softly.

'I shall feel a lot better when I've recovered from the shock,' she replied. 'That water was so cold!'

Adam hurried along to the house, carrying Justin as if he weighed no more than a feather. The front door was opened by Turner as they ascended the terrace steps.

'Is he dead?' Turner demanded, craning forward to look at Justin's face.

Adam did not reply and crossed the hall to ascend the stairs quickly, mounting them two at a time.

'He's all right,' Sarah informed Turner, and hurried after Adam.

She was aware that her feet were frozen, and looked down to see that she was barefoot but could not remember what had happened to her shoes.

'Go and get your wet clothes off and take a bath,' Adam commanded her. 'I'll see to Justin, and I won't leave him before you return.'

Sarah nodded and went into her room. She felt overwhelmingly weary as she ran a bath and then stripped off her sodden clothes. The hot water restored her quickly, but she continued to shiver spasmodically even after she had dressed in dry clothes.

She went into Justin's room to find him sitting on the bed in his dressing-gown, sipping a cup of cocoa. Adam was seated in a chair beside the bed, a hot drink in his hands. He smiled at her and motioned to a tray on the table.

'Feeling better now? Have some cocoa and it will warm you inside. Justin has been telling me again what happened. It seems the rail had worked loose. Now you're here I'm going to check on it.'

'I want to go with you, to see for myself,' Sarah said firmly.

'I'm coming, too.' Justin spoke determinedly. 'I'm all right now.'

'No.' Sarah shook her head. 'You can get out your chemistry set in the library and we'll have Janet keep an eye on you until I get back.'

They took Justin down to the library, where Adam summoned Wenn and gave the butler instructions for Justin to be watched by Janet. When the maid arrived in the library she was ordered not to let Justin out of her sight for an instant, and Sarah extracted a promise from Justin that he would not attempt to stray.

'So what do you think happened at the river?' Adam asked as he and Sarah left the house.

'We'll know more after examining that rail.' Sarah shook her head.

'Before we look at the woodwork on the bridge I must tell you that it was all checked thoroughly as a matter of routine only a month ago.' Adam's voice was filled with doubt. 'Everything like that is checked at least once a year. I just hope my suspicions are wrong otherwise I shall have to inform the police and let them investigate.'

They walked on in silence until they

reached the bridge. Sarah saw her coat and shoes lying on the river bank, where she had thrown them off, and the sight of them chilled her.

'No damage there,' Adam reported, shaking his head, 'but I would have expected the screws to have been wrenched out of the end of the rail by Justin's weight. They have gone, but the woodwork's not damaged. It looks to me as if they were removed beforehand.' He walked to the next post along, where the rail had broken under Justin's weight. 'Look at that.'

He showed Sarah the edge of the rail where it had snapped, and she saw a clean cut in the woodwork for at least half its width.

'This confirms my worst fears.' Adam sighed heavily. 'The rail has been tampered with — sawn into where it joins the post — and broke under pressure, as it was intended to. The cut is quite new. But who would do such a thing? Everyone knows this is Justin's favourite spot.'

'Can you be sure?' Sarah suppressed a shiver.

'It looks obvious to me, but I'll have a word with the estate carpenter. He's the man who carries out the annual checks.' Adam looked at Sarah, his face deadly serious, his eyes betraying the shock he was feeling. 'I don't think we should tell anyone about this,' he said softly. 'Let me check it out before we make any decision about what to do.'

'You'll tell Howard, surely.'

'I will, because he'll learn of it from someone. The staff will talk about it, certainly. Turner asked if Justin was dead the moment he opened the door to us, as if he had been expecting something bad to happen.'

'Perhaps not.' Sarah shook her head. 'You were carrying Justin, who seemed quite lifeless.'

'Go back to the house and don't let Justin out of your sight for a moment.' Adam picked up Sarah's discarded coat and shoes and handed them to her.

She experienced a wave of shock that

tremored through her, and a sudden blackness passed across her eyes. Her ears buzzed with a rush of blood through her temples and her equilibrium was affected.

She staggered and began to fall, but Adam had been watching her and caught her deftly, as if he had been expecting the incident. His strong arms encircled her and he swung her up off her feet and held her close to his chest. Sarah closed her eyes, surrendering herself to the nauseous feeling as sight and sound diminished.

'It's all right.' Adam's voice sounded as if it came from a great distance. 'You're badly shocked.'

The strength of his arms around her gave Sarah a measure of great comfort, and the weakness she experienced receded by degrees until she was able to lift her head from his shoulder. She opened her eyes to find his gaze upon her, his expression registering concern.

'Feeling better now? You're looking very pale. I shouldn't have allowed you to leave the house so soon.'

'I shall be all right now,' she responded. 'It's just a reaction to what happened.'

Adam set her feet back on the ground and supported her until she had regained her equilibrium. He held her arm as they walked back towards the house. He paused when they reached the terrace and turned to face her, looking down into her upturned face. He shook his head slowly.

'I'm sorry I've been too busy this past week to spare any time for Justin. I was looking forward to accompanying the two of you elsewhere but I just couldn't make it.'

'I thought you were distancing yourself deliberately.' Sarah spoke before she could weigh her words. 'It seemed you were avoiding me.'

Adam shook his head slowly.

'I must confess that is true.' His voice strengthened. 'Has Howard said anything to you about my apparent interest in you?'

'No.' Sarah frowned.

'He spoke to me after we returned from Shepton, and seemed to know all about our little jaunt. I suspect Elizabeth told him.' His tone hardened. 'I haven't tackled her about it but I will. Anyway, Howard warned me against showing too much interest in you and ordered me to stay away. That's why I've been so remote this past week, and I didn't enjoy the experience one bit.'

Sarah swayed and he caught her deftly, fearing she would fall. Adam held her close, his cold cheek pressing against hers. She closed her eyes, thrilled by the experience, her entire body throbbing as blood surged through her veins.

Then she opened her eyes and, glancing over Adam's shoulder, saw Elizabeth gazing at them through a drawing-room window. She gasped the information to Adam but, by the time he turned to look, Elizabeth had gone.

They entered the house and went to the library to find Justin hunched over his chemistry set. Janet looked relieved at their entrance and departed quickly. Justin looked up at them enquiringly, his features pale and strained, but his voice was remarkably firm when he spoke.

'Did you find anything?' he asked.

Adam spoke casually. 'The rail had rotted where it was screwed to the post. It was unfortunate that you were the one who leaned on it at that moment.'

Justin shook his head in disbelief.

'So it was just another of those accidents that keep happening to me. Are you sure you're not keeping anything from me? I'm old enough to be told the situation.'

'You must put it behind you now.' Adam's tone was casual, but Sarah could tell by his eyes that he was greatly concerned. She realised that she was regarding him quite differently since his confession outside. 'The question is do we tell Grandfather about the accident?'

'I think we should keep quiet about

it,' Justin said. 'But I think the way it happened was planned to catch me out. Everyone knows that bridge is my favourite spot, and I can remember seeing the carpenter checking the woodwork only a month ago.'

'I'm going to talk to the carpenter now.' Adam turned to leave. 'I'll come back and talk to you again later.'

9

The knowledge that such murderous intentions against Justin were being harboured by a member of his family filled Sarah with great disquiet. She was still being affected by the shock of the incident at the river, and a strange restlessness filled her as she tried to contain it.

Also, she could not get Adam out of her mind. Disturbing thoughts of him spread through her as she watched Justin closely. The boy seemed to be suffering little effect now of the immersion, and she wondered at his resilience.

She was startled when the door of the library was thrust open, and looked up quickly, expecting to see Adam. Disappointment filled her when Owen walked into the room, and she stifled her feelings. Owen's face was expressing shock, and he came to where she was watching Justin doing an experiment with his chemistry set.

'I can't believe what I've just heard.' Owen spoke in a hollow tone. 'Justin fell into the river and you dived in and rescued him. Is that right?'

'That's what happened.' Sarah nodded.

'Have you reported the incident to Grandfather?' Owen glanced at Justin but showed little interest in what the boy was doing. 'He'll accuse you of not taking proper care of Justin.'

'He can hardly go that far, considering I saved Justin.'

'Come over to the window. I want to talk to you.'

Owen moved away and, after pausing to consider, Sarah followed him. They walked out of earshot of Justin, who paid no attention to them.

'I'd like to accompany you the next time you take Justin away from the house.' Owen's voice contained a note that grated harshly. 'I don't think you should go out unaccompanied after this.'

'Why not? Do you think I am not capable of taking care of Justin?'

'It's not that.' He shook his head emphatically. 'It seems that someone is intent on hurting Justin, and the attempts against him may not be confined to the manor. It would be easy for an accident to occur away from the place.'

'Do you have any idea who might be planning such a thing?'

Sarah eyed him critically, noting that he was labouring under a great deal of stress. His eyes were over-bright and his hands trembled.

'Take no notice of my condition.' He seemed to know what she was thinking. 'It's caused by the tablets I have to take. When are you going out again?'

'We have no immediate plans. I'll let you know when we decide.'

'Has Adam made a point of accompanying you? He went with you to Shepton last week, and I didn't know anything about that until afterwards. You should be careful of Adam. Do you know who would inherit the estate if anything happened to Justin?'

'Yes, but I have no reason to suspect Adam any more than I would suspect you. In fact, I should think Adam has cleared himself by the way he acted when he saw us in the river. He pulled me out, undoubtedly saving my life, and I shall be eternally grateful to him.'

'Have you any suspicions regarding other members of the family?'

Sarah shook her head. 'I'm only a tutor not a detective.'

'It isn't your job to have to rescue Justin from every little scrape he gets into.' Owen turned away, then paused as an afterthought occurred to him. 'Was it an accident or had the rail on the bridge been tampered with?'

'You seem remarkably well informed about the incident,' Sarah observed.

'Turner saw it from one of the front windows and told me about it.'

Sarah caught her breath. Turner again! She suppressed a sigh and remained silent until Owen had left the room. When the door closed loudly behind him she wandered around the large room, glancing at some of the titles of the many books lining the walls, and finally paused at a window to gaze out over the rolling parkland that surrounded the house on all sides.

When the door opened again, some two hours later, Sarah looked round to see Adam entering, and her heartbeat quickened at the sight of him.

'I've been with Len Micklewight, the estate carpenter, checking over the footbridge,' Adam said curtly, and shook his head. 'It's not conclusive, I'm afraid. When Len first saw the rail he was certain it had been cut deliberately, but while we were prowling around and checking out the rest of it, he remembered that he sawed some lengths of wood, using that rail as a temporary workbench, and it is possible that he cut part the way through it. We checked out the rest of the footbridge very thoroughly and found no other defects.'

Sarah compressed her lips. She had been hoping that he would be able to prove whether or not the damage to the rail was deliberate.

'If we work together we should be able to get on top of this business. I have to get down to some estate work now,' Adam said.

Sarah told Adam of Owen's approach and how Turner had witnessed the accident from a window.

'Do you think Turner knew about the rail and was watching to see if anything would happen when he reached the footbridge? In any case, he didn't raise an alarm after seeing what happened. He apparently carried on without a second thought.'

'I'll have a word with Turner when I can get around to him.'

Adam glanced at Justin, who was engrossed with his experiment, and turned to depart.

Sarah uttered a long sigh as she considered. Time seemed to be dragging. They went to the dining-room for lunch, and she was disappointed when Adam failed to appear.

'What would you like to do this afternoon?'

She put the question to Justin as they left the dining-room.

'I think I'll lie down. I'm not feeling very well.'

Justin put a hand to his head and sighed.

Sarah frowned and placed a hand on his forehead.

'How exactly do you feel?'

'I think I'm suffering from the effects of falling into the river. I need to sleep it off.'

'Perhaps we'd better get you checked over by a doctor. Come on. You must get into bed and then I'll have a word with Adam about calling the doctor.'

'I don't need a doctor. Just let me lie down for a while.'

They went up to Justin's room. He threw himself on the bed and closed his eyes resolutely.

'You'll feel better if you undress and

get into bed,' Sarah observed.

'I'll be all right. I just want to close my eyes. I don't feel so bad now I'm lying down. Don't talk any more. I want to sleep.'

'I shall lock you in while I locate Adam,' Sarah told him.

She locked his door on the inside and went into her own room to lock the connecting door. Then she locked her own door on leaving and pocketed the keys. As she descended the stairs she met Turner ascending, and paused to talk to him.

'Owen tells me you witnessed the accident this morning,' she challenged.

'That's right.' There was an alertness about the footman that was all too plain to Sarah's discerning gaze.

'And you didn't do anything about it?'

'There was no point. I saw Adam running towards the river as you dived in. You pushed Justin into the boat and then Adam pulled you out on to the jetty. Everything was under control.'

Sarah descended the staircase and met Owen in the hall. He was wearing a topcoat.

'I'm going into Shepton,' he said. 'Would you like to come along?'

'I can't.' She told him about Justin. 'I think we should call in a doctor to him.'

'Talk to Wenn. He'll telephone for you.'

Sarah flinched at the unfriendliness in Owen's tone and remained motionless until he had departed. A moment later she heard a car driving away, and then the heavy silence of the big house closed in on her.

She was reluctant to talk to Wenn and, on impulse, turned to go back to her room. She ascended the stairs and saw Turner trying the doors of the unoccupied rooms on the first floor. He was going along the corridor away from her and she managed to unlock her door and get into her room without being seen.

Her thoughts seemed to have gotten

themselves into a rut, revolving endlessly around the river incident. Adam seemed certain now that they could circumvent any plot against Justin but she was not so sure. They would always be one step behind the plotter until he succeeded in his deadly quest.

Sarah decided that her only recourse was to see Howard and acquaint him with the details of Justin's fall into the river. The grim news should shock him into decisive action. He would have to inform the police and get professional help to guard Justin. To her way of thinking it would be criminally negligent to ignore the situation.

She turned to leave the room again but went instead to the door leading into Justin's room. She peered into the room and then gazed around with swiftly mounting disbelief for Justin was nowhere to be seen.

At first she thought he was in the bathroom, but that was empty, and she stood at the foot of the boy's bed and looked around, trying to come to terms with the grim fact of his disappearance while her thoughts moved swiftly. Was there a secret passage behind one of these thick walls?

She glanced towards the door of the room and the mystery was solved. A key was protruding from the lock. Sarah crossed to the door and removed the key, looking at it as if she had never seen one before. Justin had his own key. She tried the door and found it unlocked.

A terrible uncertainty filled her as she considered the situation. Had Justin professed sickness in order to deceive her? Whatever the reason for his absence, he was now at large in the big house, without protection.

She decided she had to locate Justin as quickly as possible and almost ran down to the library, hoping he had decided to use his chemistry set. She was stunned to find the library deserted and went back to the hall.

A noise at her back alerted her and she looked around to see Turner descending the stairs, his face professionally impassive. He shook his head when she asked if he had seen Justin.

'Don't tell me he's gone missing again. But don't worry. He'll show up when he's ready.'

'Would you locate Adam and tell him I can't find Justin?'

Turner nodded. 'I'll have to tell Wenn first. Take it from me that you'll be wasting your time searching for Justin. He'll reappear when he gets hungry. No-one knows the nooks the crannies of this house like Justin.'

Sarah turned away, unable to quell her terrible dread. She searched the rooms of the ground floor without success. Justin had vanished completely. She paused outside the door to Howard's study, wondering if she ought to consult the old man, then decided to talk to Adam first.

Minutes dragged by and, when Adam did not appear, Sarah could contain herself no longer. She went to check Justin's room again, hoping to find him there, but the room was empty and she searched the entire floor without success, and then passed through a doorway to ascend a narrow staircase that led up to the attics to find a corridor similar to the one below. She searched all the rooms that were not locked. There was no sign of Justin.

A solid wooden door blocked the end of the corridor and she withdrew a large bolt and opened the door to find a narrow staircase leading to a closed door at the top. She ascended swiftly and slid back a massive bolt then opened the upper door to find herself gazing out at the open roof.

A cold breeze swirled around her and she suppressed a shiver for she was not clothed for outdoors. She stepped out on to a flat area about six feet wide which formed the periphery of the roof and had a small retaining wall about eighteen inches high on its outside edge.

Sarah moved close to the wall and peered over to look down at the stone terrace many feet below. Her sense of balance whirled and she backed away swiftly, almost falling over a small stack of slates piled beside the door.

She was inclined to descend to the hall once more and wait for Adam, but a sense of duty impelled her to walk around the entire roof in case Justin had decided to conceal himself in the open air.

When she had completed the circuit without locating him, shivering in the bite of the cold wind, she discovered that the door which gave access to the roof was now closed, and refused to open despite her most strenuous efforts. She was stranded on the roof.

Anger filled her when she realised her plight, and it was directed against Justin. She was his only friend, and yet he resorted to playing tricks on her. She tried to find a spot that was sheltered from the cold wind but failed, and when rain fell steadily the stark reality of her position became apparent. She was in danger of falling victim to the elements, and might not be discovered before nightfall.

She returned to the obstinate door and renewed her attempts to open it. Unsuccessful and shivering violently, she positioned herself at a spot overlooking the terrace steps that ascended to the main entrance of the house and crouched behind the low parapet, hoping to glimpse someone she could call to for help.

Time passed, and each second seemed to linger in transit. She became stiff and cramped, and soon forced herself to her feet and walked unsteadily around the flat roof for exercise. Finally she saw the family car approaching along the driveway and hurried back to her original position above the terrace steps. She crouched behind the parapet to lean forward in the hope of attracting attention.

Owen alighted from the car and Sarah called to him. He began to ascend the terrace steps and she shouted at the top of her voice. Owen paused and looked around, as if trying to pinpoint the sound, but did not look up and continued on his way. Sarah became desperate.

She reached for a large slate and hurled it down to the terrace. It crashed on the steps several yards from Owen, and he darted aside and looked up. She waved and shouted, and relief filled her when he waved in return. He hurried into the house and Sarah tottered to the door to await his arrival.

When Owen opened the door, Sarah heard the drag of the bolt being pulled out of its socket and the cold certainty that she had been locked out deliberately sent a shudder through her chilled body. The door was pulled open and Owen, his face registering amazement, peered out at her.

'What on earth are you doing out there in such a dangerous spot?' he demanded. 'Is Justin with you?'

Sarah was shivering uncontrollably. She pushed by Owen and descended the stairs. Her legs were stiff, her knees difficult to control.

'I'll talk to you later,' she said. 'A hot bath will be necessary to thaw me out.'

Owen followed her down to the door of her room, asking a stream of questions which Sarah did not answer. She had never felt so cold before and hurried into her bathroom to set the hot tap running, then went to Justin's room to see if he had returned. She went back to the bathroom filled with disgust because he was still absent.

Stifling her emotions, she felt a great fear for the boy's safety. The fact that she had been locked out on the roof, probably to die of exposure, was worrying knowledge, for if Justin was not responsible then he could at this moment be in far worse trouble than she anticipated.

She fought down her fears as she soaked in water that was as hot as she could bear and, as her temperature returned to normal, her mind began to function fluently. She dressed hurriedly and went down to the hall, intent upon informing Howard of

Justin's disappearance.

Frank Turner was crossing the hall and he paused, grinning as she approached him.

'Have you found Justin yet?'

His eyes looked her over as if she were a specimen in a museum.

Sarah concluded that she did not like Turner at all. He was creepy, with an overt manner that filled her with uneasiness.

'Did you find Adam to tell him Justin is missing?' she countered.

'I looked for him but he's gone riding this afternoon.'

'Who told you Adam had gone riding?' Sarah gazed at him, her intuition insisting that he had locked her out on the roof. The evidence was in his eyes, and she knew it as if he had spoken the words.

'Micklewight, the carpenter. He's doing some work on the stables.'

Sarah nodded and turned away. She went to Howard's study and tapped at the door.

10

Sarah tapped at the door of the study while steeling herself to face Howard. She heard his voice bidding her enter and pushed open the door, wondering how best to break the grim news of Justin's disappearance to the old man.

Entering the room, she halted in amazement when her gaze fell upon Justin seated at the big desk beside Howard. Both were absorbed in Justin's chemistry set.

Justin did not look up at her entrance but Howard turned to her, his face wrinkling into a smile.

'Hello, Sarah,' he greeted. 'I must say I haven't enjoyed myself so much in years. It was good of you to let Justin visit me this afternoon. I wouldn't have thought it possible, but the changes are plain to see, and Justin tells me he's never had a better tutor.'

'That was very kind of him.' Sarah maintained a tight rein on her emotions. 'I found that treating Justin as a human being helped a great deal. If you're still busy with him then I won't drag him away.'

'If there's nothing important he's got to do right now then leave him with me a little longer.' Howard returned his attention to Justin.

Sarah departed, shaking her head. She could take Justin to task later over his behaviour. Her thoughts were upon the events that had taken place that afternoon. If Justin had not locked her out on the roof then who was responsible for her ordeal?

She went into the library and stood at a tall window, looking out at the parkland while her mind sought answers to the seemingly impossible mystery. There were no more than six people in the house, and one of them had to be the grim perpetrator of the mishaps attending Justin.

She wondered if Adam was manipulating her while pretending to be friendly. He had already attracted her immensely, arousing her emotions and effectively controlling her because of them.

The door of the library was thrust open suddenly and she started nervously at the intrusion, looking round to see Justin entering.

'I didn't know Grandfather could be such good company,' Justin declared as he placed his chemistry set on a corner of the table. 'Can we go into Shepton tomorrow and get some more chemicals? We've used nearly everything in the set.'

'Why did you lie to me about feeling ill?' Sarah spoke firmly. 'It was a lie, wasn't it?'

Justin lowered his gaze and his cheerfulness vanished. He shook his head.

'I did feel out of sorts,' he said. 'I thought someone had put something in my food to make me feel ill. But it went off after you left me. I looked for you but couldn't find you so I went to Grandfather because I always feel safe with him. He was interested in my chemistry set so I fetched it and we were busy with experiments until you showed up.'

'I returned to your room within minutes of leaving you, found you absent without good cause, and assumed something bad had happened to you.' Sarah's tone was severe. 'I searched the entire house for you, except for the study because I didn't want to alarm Howard unnecessarily. I even went up to the roof in case you had decided to risk your life up there.'

'I was all right. You should have looked in the study. How can you search a place without looking everywhere?'

The door was opened and Sarah looked up to see Adam in the doorway. A measure of relief filled her, but a glimpse of Adam's face sent a pang through her breast.

'I have had the most harrowing afternoon of my life,' Adam said. He gazed at Justin for some moments without saying anything more, then pulled a cap from his pocket and thrust it under Justin's nose. 'This is yours, I believe.'

Justin took the cap but Adam snatched it back, shaking his head. Sarah frowned, wondering what had occurred. Adam glanced at her with anger in his narrowed eyes.

'Has Justin been in your company all afternoon?' he demanded.

'No. He hasn't been with me at all. What's wrong?'

'Someone opened the paddock gate just after lunch and the bull got out. It reached the main road and went towards Shepton. I had to get all the estate workers out to recapture it, and one of the men broke his leg in the effort.' He fingered Justin's cap, then looked at the boy. 'Your cap was found beside the opened gate.'

'I was with Grandfather all this

afternoon,' Justin responded sullenly. 'I didn't do it. I haven't been out of the house since this morning.'

'You can't get out of it this time.' Adam spoke harshly. 'This business is too serious to be overlooked as a childish prank.'

'Do you know the precise time the animal was turned loose?' Sarah asked. 'If so then it would be a simple matter to check with Howard to ascertain the time Justin joined him in the study.'

Adam nodded. 'Wait here until I return,' he said, and turned on his heel to depart.

'I didn't do it,' Justin said earnestly. 'I was with Grandfather, honestly.'

'Someone else did it and left your cap on the spot to throw the blame on you.' Sarah spoke in a neutral tone.

'I've always been blamed for things I didn't do.'

'I was locked out on the roof this afternoon when I ventured there in search of you,' she mused. 'I thought immediately that you were the culprit but apparently you were with Howard.'

'I wouldn't have done that to you.' Justin shook his head emphatically. 'I might have done it to some of my other tutors but you saved my life.'

Sarah sighed as she shook her head.

'Justin, there is a cloud of uncertainty surrounding you. I've been here over a week now, and I can't believe half of what I've seen. No-one is checking out this situation properly, or with the caution it warrants. Personally I don't know what to believe any more.'

'I don't know what to say.' Justin grimaced.

Adam returned at that moment, still angered by his experiences of the afternoon but his ire was no longer directed at Justin. He held out Justin's cap and the boy took it.

'Grandfather bears out your story and, according to his recollection of the time you joined him, I'm certain you couldn't have turned the bull loose.' Adam rubbed his chin. 'I'm sorry, Justin, but it looked black for you.

However, if you didn't open the paddock gate then who did?'

'Before you go on to consider that imponderable you'd better learn what happened to me this afternoon.' Sarah related her experience on the roof, and saw Adam's eyes narrow as he listened.

There was a tap at the door and it was opened. Wenn stepped into the doorway.

'Excuse me, Mr Adam. There's a policeman here to see you.'

'Thank you, Wenn. I'll be along in a moment.' Adam waited until the butler closed the door. 'We cannot go into this now. The police were informed that the bull was loose, and they'll want a statement from me about that. We need to get together on this, Sarah, for it seems to have fallen to us to take the initiative.

'I don't want to talk in the house. These walls have ears. Meet me in my office in the stable block after dinner this evening.'

Sarah agreed, nodding. 'I'll be there.'

Adam departed and Justin clutched at Sarah's arm.

'This concerns me,' he said urgently. 'I want to be there this evening and hear what you and Adam decide.'

Sarah smiled and shook her head.

'I don't think so. What you should be concentrating on is making it difficult for anyone to get at you. In future you'd better stay close to me, or keep me informed of your whereabouts.'

She paused and considered for a moment.

'I would like to know why you felt you had to lie to me about feeling ill in order to spend time with your grandfather. If you had asked properly I would not have refused, and I would have known where you were.'

'I'm sorry. I didn't lie about how I felt. I was feeling sick, and it must have been the shock of falling into the river. When it passed off you were gone, and I didn't like being on my own.'

'Let's try and put all thoughts of what's been happening right out of our

157

minds,' Sarah said firmly. 'What shall we do now to fill in our time?'

The door was opened before Justin could reply and Janet appeared.

'Mr Howard would like to see you in his study, miss,' the maid announced.

'You'll have to come with me, Justin.' Sarah walked to the door. 'I'm not letting you out of my sight for a single moment.'

Justin grinned and hurried to open the door for her. They went to the study. Sarah tapped at the door and Justin opened it when they heard Howard's invitation to enter.

'I want to talk to you alone,' Howard said sharply. 'Run along, Justin. Wait for Sarah in the library.'

'Stay here, Justin,' Sarah responded. 'I'm sorry, Howard, but I won't let Justin out of my sight.'

Howard paused, surprised by her attitude. Then he shrugged.

'Very well. Sit down by the fire, Justin.' He sighed and shook his head. 'I've just learned of the incident at the river. I can't imagine how you could have been so foolhardy as to allow Justin to place himself in such peril. I'm deeply shocked that he came so very near to drowning.'

'Sarah dived in and rescued me,' Justin said sharply. 'You should be thanking her, Grandfather, not blaming her.'

'Who told you about the incident?' Sarah asked.

'That's neither here nor there. I'm incensed because I wasn't informed immediately. Why was it kept from me?'

'To spare you from the shock of it all. Adam and I thought if better to conceal the incident. Justin is none the worse for what happened and we are now on our guard.' Sarah drew a deep breath. 'I must insist that you tell me who informed you of the incident.'

'Why is that so important?' Howard's dark eyes were like gimlets boring into Sarah. 'In view of what's happening I think I should terminate your employment immediately. Perhaps a male tutor would be more suitable.'

Justin sprang to his feet.

'I won't have another tutor,' he said firmly. 'Sarah is the best tutor I've ever had, and she saved my life this morning. Why are you blaming her?'

'Be quiet, Justin. I am not blaming Sarah for anything, but a mere woman cannot be expected to handle such difficulties.'

'I'm no longer alone,' Sarah said. 'Adam is backing me.'

'Adam has too much to do with running the estate.' Howard shook his head. He turned and paced the room several times, hands clasped behind his back and eyes gazing at the floor. Sarah watched him in silence, filled with dismay at his decision to dispense with her services. Justin was looking grim as he watched Howard.

'If you send Sarah away I shall run away,' Justin said finally.

Howard ceased his pacing and ran his fingers through his wispy hair. He shook his head sorrowfully, and Sarah could see that worry was piling an intolerable burden on his bowed shoulders.

'I'm meeting with Adam this evening,' Sarah said. 'After this morning's incident we have come to terms with the situation. At first it was impossible to face up to it because it is too shocking to accept that someone in this house is determined to harm Justin. But the fact remains, and if you will not call in the police then we must unmask the guilty person ourselves and deliver him to you.'

'Very well.' Howard nodded. 'I'll refrain from a decision until you've talked to Adam.'

11

Sarah's nerves began to stretch as the time to meet Adam in the stable block drew nigh. She had managed to get Janet to sit with Justin, and left them together when she set out, carrying a small pocket torch. She experienced qualms at leaving Justin but a sense of eagerness inside her at the thought of seeing Adam smoothed over her fears.

Sarah opened the front door, switched on the torch, and stepped out into the blustery night, being swallowed up immediately by intense darkness. Thankful for the torch, she hurried along the path leading around the house.

The leafless branches of trees whipped and flailed maliciously under the force of the gusting wind. Rain slashed down in a sudden furious outburst, its insistent sound forming a sinister background to the wild October night.

She reached the rear of the house and paused when dim light relieved the darkness ahead. Relief filled her when she realised that she was looking at the estate office.

A figure moved in the shadows beside the entrance and Sarah paused uncertainly, then Adam spoke and she hurried forward.

'Hello,' he greeted. 'I was wondering if you would come. It's a bit of a liberty, dragging you away from Justin at this time.'

'I don't mind,' she responded. 'I've left him with Janet.'

He led her inside the building and they entered a large, comfortable office. Sarah looked around with interest as Adam showed her to a seat and then went behind the desk and sat down facing her.

'This is a very difficult situation,' he said softly. 'The question is who is responsible for the incidents befalling

Justin? I've spent the past week observing everyone in the manor. Initially I suspected Owen, and watched him very closely. I know Elizabeth doesn't like Justin because of the way he acts but that doesn't put her into the class of person we are seeking. I've even suspected Howard on the odd occasion.'

'I know exactly what you mean.' Sarah nodded. 'I have been watching points myself and I'm no nearer a solution than you.'

Adam nodded. 'It's getting to the point where I'm convinced that the only thing to do is call in the police and let them make an investigation.'

'Why would anyone turn the bull loose and put the blame on Justin?' Sarah mused. 'The other incidents I can understand. Someone wants to get rid of the boy — but getting him blamed for opening a gate doesn't make sense.'

'I think it was done as a final straw. Every time something bad happens and

Justin is blamed for it, Grandfather considers sending him away from here to be educated.'

Sarah moved uneasily in her seat and said, 'Whoever is at the bottom of it doesn't make mistakes, and if Justin is sent away he wouldn't stand a chance on his own.'

'Let me think about it.' Adam arose then and Sarah got to her feet. 'I can see that we won't make further progress just by talking so I'd better see you back to the house and then return to wade through this paperwork.' He indicated the pile of papers on the desk.

'I can find my own way back to the house,' she replied, disappointed by the short time she had been in his company. She turned towards the door. 'Don't worry about me.'

'That's the problem.' He sighed heavily. 'I do worry about you, and a great deal more than shows. I never get enough time to attend to personal affairs. It's all work and no play for me.'

Sarah paused and turned to face him,

intrigued by his tone, and suddenly they were very close. Adam halted abruptly as she stopped unexpectedly but they made contact inadvertently. Sarah recoiled and almost lost her balance, and Adam's arms lifted swiftly, grasping her elbows to steady her.

Time seemed to stand still as she looked up into his face. His expression changed as he loomed over her, and she heard the catch in his breath as a strange hunger expressed itself in his eyes. His hands tightened convulsively and then moved from her elbows and slid around her shoulders to embrace her.

'I'm very worried about you,' he said softly.

Sarah leaned in against him, keenly aware of the burden bearing down upon her mind.

Adam put a hand under her chin and tilted her face up towards him. She closed her eyes as he kissed her, and was inundated by a surge of conflicting passions. Then reality struck her like an arrow and she drew back from him.

'I'm sorry,' he said at once. 'I shouldn't have done that.'

Sarah quashed the impulse to thrust herself back into his arms and shook her head as passionate urges tremored through her.

'I agree,' she said reluctantly. 'I'd better go.'

She departed quickly, aware that her feelings corresponded with the emotion Adam had displayed. Her mind was in turmoil as she left the office and retraced her steps along the path towards the house.

An unnatural sound in the under-growth just behind her pulled her up in mid-stride. She looked around quickly, swinging the beam of the torch to check her surroundings. She heard a muffled oath as someone sprawled somewhere in the shadows.

Sarah saw nothing and switched off the torch. She ran several paces along the path, heard what sounded like pursuit, and stepped sideways off the path to fade into the darkness. A furtive shadow slipped by her.

She gripped the torch and followed cautiously. The figure went to the back door. Sarah craned forward as the door was opened and light issued from the kitchen to illuminate a figure huddled in a black coat. Rain slashed into her face but she saw enough to recognise Frank Turner. The footman hurried inside and closed the door quickly.

Sarah had to ring the bell because the front door was locked, and anxious moments passed before the door was opened by Turner, who had already divested himself of his coat. His hair looked windswept and there were spots of rain on his face. He seemed uneasy, but forced a smile at the sight of her.

'I hope it was worth it, going out on a night like this,' he observed.

'I'm still on duty,' Sarah responded. 'But what took you out?'

'Me!' Turner shook his head. 'I haven't been out. Wild horses couldn't drag me out on a night like this.'

'Why are you lying? You were outside the stable block while I was in the estate office talking to Adam. I heard you, and saw you enter the house by the back door.'

Turner's face had paled at her accusation and his eyes showed a flash of fear. 'All right, I was outside but it had nothing to do with you. I didn't know you had gone out. I met Janet outside. We've been seeing each other, and have to meet in secret because Mrs Wenn doesn't hold with members of the staff getting together.'

Sarah's eyes narrowed. 'Did you see Janet?'

'Of course.'

Turner's tone roughened and his face took on a belligerent expression.

'Janet is the one who hasn't been out this evening,' Sarah replied firmly, 'and we can verify that quite easily. I got her to stay with Justin while I slipped out and she is still with him. Come along and we'll check that it is so. I shall be interested in your real reason for lying about being outside.'

'Forget it,' he advised. 'I wouldn't want anyone else to know I've been seeing Janet on the quiet. We could both lose our jobs if it came out. You're quite right. I didn't see Janet this evening although we had arranged to meet. I didn't know you'd got her to stand in for you with Justin, and went out expecting to see her as arranged. I was coming back after waiting in vain, and that's when you saw me. It was all quite innocent.'

Sarah sensed that he was lying but nodded as if she believed him.

She turned away and began to ascend the stairs, glancing back over her shoulder when she reached the upper corridor, and was surprised to see Turner following at a distance. She hurried along to her room, and entered, locking the door at her back.

Going into Justin's room, she found him sitting by the fire, reading a book aloud to Janet, who was listening rather attentively. Justin threw down the book the instant he saw Sarah.

'Can I go now, miss?' Janet sprang to her feet.

'Yes, Janet,' Sarah countered.

Sarah followed the maid to the door and looked out into the corridor as the maid went towards the staircase. She was in time to see Turner disappearing up the stairs leading to the attic. She turned to Justin.

'Lock this door when I leave,' she instructed him, 'and don't open it to anyone but me. I have to check out something that could be very important. I won't be long. Can I trust you to remain here?'

'Yes.' Justin nodded. 'I'm too afraid now to wander around on my own.'

Sarah hurried along the corridor in pursuit of Turner. She mounted the attic stairs silently and peered along the upper passage without revealing herself. Turner was standing at a door on the right, which was open, and he was talking loudly to someone inside the attic room.

'I tell you it's not my imagination,' the footman was saying. 'She's definitely suspicious of me. I had to think fast to find an excuse to put her off. You'll have to do something about her. Give me the money you owe me and I'll be a long way from here by morning.'

'Don't be ridiculous,' a man's voice replied in a low tone.

Sarah strained to recognise the voice. Her first thought was that it was Owen, then Francis emerged from the room and Turner moved back from him. Sarah stared in amazement at Elizabeth's husband as he lifted a hand in a threatening gesture to the footman.

'You can't leave,' Francis rasped. 'You're in too deep. We've got to see it through to the bitter end, and there's no money for anyone if we don't succeed, so don't try to squeeze me.'

'You said it would be easy to arrange an accident that would get rid of Justin, but there have been too many incidents as it is. No-one would stand for another. Sarah is clearly suspicious. I don't care what you say, I'm handing in my notice in the morning, and I don't want anything else to do with your schemes.'

'Go and fetch Sarah up here.' Francis spoke hoarsely. He seemed to be under great stress. 'I have been saving the ultimate solution in case everything else failed. We haven't gone this far just to give up when another effort will succeed,' he snarled. 'Don't forget that you weakened the bridge rail. That was attempted murder. How long do you think you'll get in prison if that came out?'

'What are you going to do?' Turner persisted.

'A fire is the perfect solution.' Francis pushed Turner along the corridor towards the stairs. 'Get going and fetch Sarah. Then you can go back for Justin. I'll lock them in an attic room and set fire to it.'

'You'll burn the house down!' Turner protested. 'You want the estate for Elizabeth, but if you burn the house there'll be nothing left.'

'Insurance will rebuild the house.'

Francis pushed Turner towards the stairs.

Sarah listened with horror piling up in her mind. She could not believe what she was hearing, and when Turner came towards the stairs she descended quickly, intent on getting Justin and running to Adam for help. In her haste she overbalanced and sprawled, landing in a heap in the lower corridors. She struck her head and was dazed.

Turner pounced on her before she could recover, his strong hands dragging her upright.

'Up the stairs,' Turner rapped, thrusting her forward. 'I need money from Francis before I can go anywhere.'

Sarah was compelled to obey, and Turner held her arm as they ascended the stairs. He thrust her into the room which Francis used as a studio. There were paintings lining the walls and stacks of canvases standing around.

A tall easel was positioned before a

large window. An oil lamp was standing on a desk in a corner of the room — there was no electricity laid on in any of the attic rooms. Francis got up from the desk and came towards Sarah, scowling.

'So you've been snooping' he accused. 'Well, there's only one way to deal with you.' He grasped her arm and turned on Turner. 'What are you waiting for? Go and get the boy.'

Sarah faced Francis with a show of courage she was far from feeling.

'You must be mad if you think you can kill Justin and me, then get rid of Adam and Owen, for that's what you'll have to do if Elizabeth is to inherit.'

Francis pushed her and she staggered backwards against the desk with such violence that the oil lamp toppled to the floor. Francis sprang forward, hands outstretched, to catch the lamp, but missed it by inches. Glass shattered as the lamp thudded on the floor and burning oil spread quickly.

Francis yelled and darted backwards

as oil splashed his shoes, which became engulfed in flames. He stamped across the floor and departed quickly before Sarah could think of escaping, slamming the door and bolting it on the outside. Sarah felt the first pangs of fear envelop her.

The fire was spreading quickly. Sarah looked around for some means of beating at the flames but there was nothing suitable in the room.

Sarah ran to the door and tried to force it open but it was stoutly built and she failed to budge it. She gazed in horror at the swiftly growing fire, then ran to the window and tried to open it, until she saw that it had been nailed down.

Her fear increased when she realised she was trapped. She returned to the door and hammered on the stout panels in a vain hope that someone might hear and come to investigate, but only the hollow echoes of the din she created resounded through the deep silence enveloping the attic. Despair filled her as she realised the futility of the situation.

The sound of the bolt being withdrawn on the outside of the door made her retreat to the centre of the room. The door swung open, and she gaped in shock at Justin, who stood peering into the room. She ran to him, pushing him back into the corridor, and slammed the door at her back to prevent smoke escaping into the rest of the attic.

'What are you doing here, Justin?' she demanded.

'Turner knocked on my door but I wouldn't open it. He told me you had fallen down the attic stairs and said I should come to you while he telephoned for help. When I opened my door he grabbed me and brought me up here, then bolted the door on the other side. I heard you banging in here so I opened the door. What's happening, Sarah? The studio is on fire!'

'It seems that Francis and Turner have been responsible for your accidents,' Sarah replied. 'And we're trapped in here, Justin, unless we can find a way down.'

'There is a way out,' Justin said eagerly. 'There's a fire escape outside the window at the end of this passage.'

Justin ran to the end of the corridor and tugged at the window catch but could not open the window. Sarah grasped the catch, exerted her strength and the catch moved. She thrust up the window and peered outside.

Rain lashed into her face but she saw an iron fire escape fixed outside the window. She climbed out on to the platform and grasped the rail. Justin followed her nimbly and they descended slowly to the lower floors.

They reached the platform at the window on the first floor and Sarah paused to look into the room, which was lighted. She saw Owen lying on the bed in the room, his inert position suggesting that he had imbibed too much drink, as usual. She rapped on the window but Owen did not respond.

'We must get down quickly,' Sarah

gasped. 'We have to get to Adam and raise the alarm.'

They continued down the escape, and Sarah was immensely relieved when they reached the ground. She grasped Justin's hand and hurried him away towards the stable.

Despair filled her when she saw the stable block was in complete darkness. She had counted on Adam being here.

'Justin, you wait in Adam's office while I go back to the house,' she demanded.

'They might come after me,' he replied fearfully.

'They don't know you're out here. They think you're up in the attic.'

'I'll try it,' Justin replied. 'Adam usually locks the office door but I know how to get the window open. It's round here.'

He led the way along a dark wall and then reached up. Sarah could not see what he was doing, but heard the window creak open. Justin climbed up on to the sill and disappeared into the office.

She saw a light in Howard's study and went to the window, where the curtains were undrawn. Howard was sitting in an easy chair before the fire, dozing, and he started up quickly when Sarah rapped on the window.

She knocked furiously until he realised where the sound was coming from, and it took him several moments to come to the window, his face registering amazement when he saw Sarah standing outside.

Howard opened the window and Sarah climbed in over the sill. The old man gazed at her wordlessly, almost unable to believe his eyes.

'I'm sorry but there's no way I can spare you from this shock,' she said breathlessly. 'The house is on fire. It started in the attic. We must raise the alarm.'

He was quick to realise the import of her words and staggered to the study door, where a bell rope was suspended. He tugged the rope and Sarah sighed with relief as she explained what she had learned of the plot Francis had planned.

'I'll get everyone out of the house if you'll telephone the fire brigade in Shepton,' she suggested, and Howard moved dazedly to the telephone.

At that moment Wenn appeared from the kitchen. The butler evinced no emotion when Sarah explained the situation.

'We must evacuate the house immediately,' he said.

'Have you seen Adam?' she demanded. 'He's not in the estate office.'

'I let him into the house about ten minutes ago,' Wenn reported. 'He went up to his room, I believe.'

'Take care of Howard,' Sarah gasped. 'He's badly shocked. Owen is lying on the bed in his room. He looks as if he'll need help to move.'

Sarah ascended the staircase hurriedly and ran towards Owen's room. She was horrified to see smoke filling the end of the corridor, seeping down under the door leading to the attic.

She opened the door of Owen's room, calling his name frantically. Owen was still lying on his bed, unmoving, and she hurried to his side and grasped his arm, shaking him violently. His eyes flickered open and he looked up at her with a little animation.

'The house is on fire,' she gasped. 'Come on, Owen, pull yourself together. You have to get out now.'

'You're wasting your time,' Turner said from the doorway. 'He's drunk himself insensible.'

Sarah spun to face the door, and a gasp escaped her. Turner lunged at her, his face expressing desperation.

'You think you're very clever getting out of the attic,' he snarled. 'Francis expected Justin to show you the way. He guessed you would put Justin somewhere safe before venturing into the house to raise the alarm and was waiting for you to reach the ground because he couldn't risk bringing the boy down through the house. Right now he's probably got hold of Justin.

The boy is going into the river, and you will join him when I get you out so don't give me any trouble.'

He lunged at her and Sarah screamed. Turner raised a hand to strike her. Sarah tried to duck away, and then Turner was pulled away from her and she saw Adam in the doorway. He thrust Turner against the wall so hard the footman fell to the floor.

'What is going on?' Adam demanded.

She explained in a halting voice, her eyes upon the hapless Turner, who was shaking his head. The footman suddenly sprang up and ran out of the room. Adam was shaken by the revelation and turned quickly to rouse Owen. At that moment Wenn came into the room.

'I'll take care of Mr Owen,' Wenn said. 'Everyone else is leaving the house. The fire brigade is on its way from Shepton.'

'We must get to your office in the stables,' Sarah said urgently.

They went down to the back door

and Adam jerked it open. Sarah was only yards behind him as he ran along the darkened path towards the stable block. She was horrified to see lights in the stable and feared that they were too late.

Francis had plotted only too well. Then she heard Justin's voice crying out in terror and pushed herself to the limit to keep up with Adam, who surged forward but missed his footing and sprawled heavily. Sarah passed him and kept going, driven by extreme concern for Justin.

The door to the office was open. Sarah reached the doorway and saw Francis struggling with Justin, trying to subdue the boy. She paused in the doorway, gasping for breath, and Francis saw her and released Justin, who shrank back into a corner.

'You again.' Francis came forward swiftly, hands reaching for Sarah.

Sarah felt a strong hand on her shoulder and she was pulled out of the doorway. Adam passed her, big, strong and protective. Francis paused, shaken by Adam's unexpected appearance, but Adam was under no illusions.

He stepped forward a short pace and his right fist swung in a powerful arc. The sound of his knuckles connecting with his brother-in-law's chin was sharp in the close confines of the office. Francis fell to the floor and lay still.

'Get Justin out of here,' Adam said. 'I can handle this.'

Justin skirted the prostrate Francis and ran to Sarah, but Adam grasped Sarah's shoulder as she led Justin away.

'Before we go any further,' he said. 'Now it's all over there's something I need to do before the opportunity passes.'

Sarah gazed at him wordlessly and he took her into his arms, kissing her hungrily. She responded wholeheartedly, filled with an overwhelming relief because now, the nightmare had ended.